Frozen Beauty

BOOKS 1-3

By

Steve Turnbull

For Eddie

CONTENTS

The Chinese Vase..7

Ladies' Day 73

Dr Morbury's Cargo 163

BOOK 1

THE CHINESE VASE

1

Qi Zang tightened the belt of the heavy, too-large coat wrapped around her slim frame. There was no point spending money on one that fitted when it performed its function sufficiently well. Besides, she only required it when inspecting the cargo. She rotated the electric knob protruding from the wall, her fingertips only just peeking from the sleeve, and the lights scattered around the hold reluctantly lit up. Many were not working at all, and they had a higher priority than coats.

She scraped the frost from the wall-mounted thermometer. The reading was two degrees above freezing. Just as well they would make port today. She descended the wooden spiral staircase from the gallery into the cargo area. Her breath condensed in white clouds that did not dissipate but hung and swirled as she stepped through them.

She pulled leather gauntlets from a coat pocket and wriggled her hands into them. The hand rail was encrusted with an ice layer from the days it had taken to cross the Himalayas and come down to the northern Indian plain on the way to Delhi.

Twice daily she checked the cargo to ensure the stacked blocks of ice were lashed down firmly, and that any melt water hadn't refrozen and clogged the outlets. A small ship like the *Frozen Beauty* didn't have crew to spare. As captain she was responsible for the cargo, whether it was the ice bound for the houses of the westerners and for meat storage or—she glanced towards the far end of the hold—any of the other cargo.

It hadn't been a bad run this time, though autumn was best. Even while it was still summer here at low altitudes they could head up into Tibet, avoiding the trigger-happy Chinese soldiers in their forts, just as the ice was freezing on the lakes. They could have a profitable journey in less than three weeks. And still get back for one or two further trips.

Other times of the year they might be able to get the ice, but it was harder to cut in winter and harder to find in summer so they supplemented their income in other ways. Contracting to carry ice for one of the big companies would barely cover their costs. Independent ships had to make other arrangements for the leaner parts of the year.

She began her survey of the cargo by systematically criss-crossing the gangplanks, twanging each line in turn. She found a slack one and spent a couple of minutes retying it before moving on. The lines towards the stern frequently came loose as they were directly beneath the furnace and boiler.

None of the other lines needed her attention. Ending her survey at the forward end of the hold, she flipped off the lights and put her shoulder into getting the door open. On the third shove, the ice of accumulated hours shattered with a resounding crack. Warm air flowed past her; she went through and slammed the door. Ice was sold by weight. The less they lost the better they were paid.

* * *

Second-in-command, Dingbang Hsieh, was at the wheel as Qi pushed the door to the hold shut. He turned and smiled as she entered, then went back to watching the undulating green terrain a few hundred feet below them.

"Anything to report?"

"No bad weather. Easterly wind at ten knots."

They used English for the sake of the rest of the crew; it was the only language they all had in common. All except Ichiro, who could only talk with his hands. She looked out to starboard and saw another "ice bucket" flying down from the frozen Tibetan lakes. Its hydrogen gas bag undulated beneath its streamlining silk envelope, its rotors were a blur and it poured smoke from its single stack.

Qi stripped off the gloves, stuffed them into the coat's pockets, and hung it behind the door ready for her return trip later. They should have made it to Delhi by midday, but the strong headwind they had been experiencing had delayed them. If they arrived too late the cargo would not get unloaded until the morning which meant less profit.

She took the binoculars from their hook by the window and scanned the other ship. It was on the same heading, but with a slight lead.

"It's the *Jackanape*," said Ding without turning. Captain Klein was another independent so he and Zang would be vying to get their cargo unloaded and sold. His Australian-built ship carried less but was more streamlined, which meant it was faster—especially in this headwind.

"Otto?"

The tall, blond German boy looked up from the chart table. It had taken weeks of training to stop him from coming to attention and saluting at the slightest provocation. She did not recall ever seeing him smile, but she could be accused of the same.

"Captain, we are on course. I have calculated our arrival to be 17:00 hours."

"How many degrees off our heading is the wind?"

"10 degrees to the south, Captain."

She considered for a moment. The port at Delhi was southwest of the city. "Recalculate for a new heading directly into the wind to take us past Delhi and then turning with the wind behind us."

"Aye, Captain."

He turned away and sat at the Babbage in the corner. He pulled out a stack of fresh cards from the small cupboard, along with the hole punch. She shook her head. In the hands of a clever computationer, these Babbages were almost magic. Of course theirs had not been made by the Babbage Corporation, who supplied the British exclusively and received funding for developments. Like the rest of the *Beauty*, the computing machine had been built in Shanghai, a copy built from British patents.

She went to the helm and stood beside Ding. She had known him all her life; he had been first mate to her father before her. His presence was comforting but not like a father's: more like a mother's.

"I'll take her now."

"Aye, Captain."

Ding stepped away from the helm but kept a hand on it; she stepped into his place and placed both hands on the wheel. Ding crossed his arms and stood beside her, watching the terrain. The green of Uttar Pradesh stretched out ahead of them, sprinkled with trees, fields, and villages.

Ding had been at the helm since shortly before daybreak. Flying at night, or even early morning, in the mountains was not recommended but they could not waste what little light they had.

Behind her, the Babbage hissed as Otto opened the steam valve. The cogs turned and its clattering filled the room. They would have the answer in a few minutes, assuming Otto had not made a mistake. They would have to gain more altitude over the high plains. Only the big British ships flew at high altitude when given a choice. For everyone else bad weather was always a risk, and thunderstorms terrified captains with hydrogen-lift vessels; ordinary traders couldn't afford to buy the Americans' helium.

But the *Beauty* did not rely on dangerous hydrogen to supplement the partial gravity nullification of the Faraday device. Qi pulled the communication funnel from the wall, extracted the whistle mouthpiece and blew hard. A moment's delay stretched to several. She blew again.

"*Oui?*" The voice, piped from two decks above, came as a tinny squeak. Remy Darras could not be persuaded to indulge in any shipboard etiquette. After all—as he would say whenever given the opportunity—he was an artist, not a sailor, descended from the Montgolfier Brothers. She had not yet queried how he could be descended from both of them.

"Can we make five thousand feet, Monsieur Darras?"

"*Certainement.* We can make fifteen thousand if you desire."

"Five will be quite sufficient, if you please."

"As you wish, Madame Captain." She passed the tube to Ding, who replaced the whistle and hung it back in its place.

"Captain?"

"Yes, Otto."

"I believe we may gain thirty minutes."

"Very good. Can you recalculate this every hour?"

"Yes, Captain."

Qi smiled. There was a surge and a gentle pressure into the floor as the *Beauty* climbed. In her mind's eye she could see the seven hot-air balloons expanding as the super-heated steam pipes fed them more heat. The ground slipped away.

Hand over hand, she delicately pulled the helm to port. On the hull the steering rotors adjusted their direction and the *Beauty* responded. The world before her swung to the right; as the compass showed eight degrees of change she gently re-centred it. She looked out to starboard and watched the *Jackanape* disappearing into the distance and below them. Smiling, she ran her fingers across the helm, worn smooth by years of love.

We are not scared of heights, are we, Beauty?

2

Fanning did not know what was wrong with her. She knew there was a time when she had been perfectly well, but she couldn't remember when that was. To be fair, it was not she who thought there was something wrong; it was everybody else.

She strode through the shopping district, pulling stares from all the very proper ladies and gentlemen. She was aware that her clothes were the reason, but once again she could not fully understand why. The trousers and shirt were clean if a little old, and her boots were polished to a shine that would honour any army officer. Quite why that attracted such disapproval, she could not fathom.

She found the jewellery shop easily enough and pushed open the door. The small bell tinkled and alerted the proprietor who rose from his chair behind the counter. He was tall and dressed in a sort of black robe. The place was full of shadows; the only illumination came from the electric lights in the display cases. And each case contained finely wrought Indian silver bracelets, watches, and other jewellery. She particularly noted the eye-catching silver cuff-links with the pattern of tiny diamonds set into their surface.

"What do you want, boy?"

She pulled a small package from her pocket. "Delivery from Mrs Devonshire."

The man grunted and held out his hand. Fanning set the carefully wrapped package, hardly bigger than a snuff box, on the shopkeeper's open palm. The Chinaman pulled off the string, and unfolded the plain paper. Inside was a layer of cotton wool protecting a pair of pearl earrings in simple gold settings.

"Mrs Devonshire, is it?" He looked at her with his head to one side. The name Devonshire was used to protect the identity of the seller. "How do I know you didn't steal them?"

She met his eye. "Would I have wrapped them? In cotton wool?"

He sniffed and looked back at the earrings. "Two pounds."

"I'll have them back and go elsewhere." She put out her hand.

"And ten shillings."

"Mrs Devonshire said I should come back with at least ten pounds."

He gave a short coughing laugh. "Mrs Devonshire's new to this game, is she? I'm stealing from my own mother but I'll give you three pounds."

"Mrs Devonshire was very firm about this. Seven."

"Three pound ten. They're slightly worn and that's not best quality gold."

"Six. Those pearls are perfect."

"Four. And I'll be making a loss."

"Stealing from yourself ranks worse than stealing from your mother, old man? Five pound ten."

"I'll ask you to keep a civil tongue in your head, boy. I won't pay more than four. That's my final offer. Mrs Devonshire had better like it."

"Mrs Devonshire's husband's got no horse sense, if you catch my drift, and there'll be more of this coming your way, if I'm not much mistaken. If the price is right."

He stared into her face and frowned. "You're not a boy."

"I'll thank you to keep a civil tongue in your head, sir. Four pound ten."

"Done."

They shook hands.

* * *

The bungalows of the British elite were located on a hill in the north of the city. They were ranged around the slope with their frontages faced south while the main living areas faced north, towards the mountains, so the sun made less of an impression.

The residential houses reminded Fanning of home in a way the British municipal buildings did not. The wood bungalows with their wide balconies were raised off the ground to allow cooling air to circulate beneath. Back in Louisiana the style may have been different but the purpose was the same.

She found the house, went around back and knocked on the kitchen door.

It was opened by a young Indian maid who recognised her and let her in. Here they had Indians where back home they had blacks. Those in power always trod on someone to keep themselves out the swamp.

There was a few minutes' wait while the mistress was informed of Fanning's arrival. She took the opportunity to partake of some bread. The cook did not object, but when her back was turned Fanning pocketed a few more fresh rolls.

The maid returned and escorted her through to a living room with some very good quality but worn furniture. The lady stood by the fireplace. It was laid for a fire but unlit, and would probably stay like that most of the year. Mrs Cameron was probably in her late twenties but she looked much older: the price of a wastrel husband.

"Miss Fanning," the lady said.

She hated it when they referred to her as a girl even though she understood on one level that was how she looked. Regardless, it was important to remain polite with one's clients. "Just 'Fanning', if you please, Mrs Cameron."

"I'm sorry, I forgot." She sighed delicately and turned to face Fanning. "You managed to…"—she searched for an appropriate word—"conduct the business?"

"Certainly, ma'am." Fanning reached into her pocket, withdrew four pound notes and handed them over. The lady counted them.

"So little," she sighed again and extracted one of the notes, offering it back.

"No, ma'am. I have already taken my tithe." She displayed the four half-crowns before shoving them back into her pocket. Mrs Cameron nodded sadly and tucked the notes into her bodice. "I know it ain't my place, Mrs Cameron. But maybe you should ditch that husband of yours."

The lady had a pretty smile when she wore it; that probably didn't happen too often. "And where would I go? How would I live?"

"Seems to me there's not much that could be worse than selling your precious things, just because your husband always backs the slowest ponies." Fanning took a step forward and grasped the woman's hand. She did not pull away. "You say the word, Mrs Cameron, and I will carry you away from this."

"You are very kind, but it cannot be."

Fanning bowed and lifted her fingers to her lips. "You know where to find me if you need another transaction, or another life."

And with that Fanning turned and left.

3

At five thousand feet the view from the open deck was majestic. To the north, the Himalayas highlighted the horizon with a band of brilliant white. The flood plain was a green swathe interrupted by the thick smog of Delhi that streamed away east in the wind. To the south lay the mountains of Rajasthan. The ship had passed equidistant between Delhi and Jaipur twenty-five minutes earlier and was due for the turn.

Qi had been correct. By turning into the wind the ship offered less resistance and could thus travel faster. In addition they did not have to waste steam compensating for wind-drift. Now they would turn into Delhi with the wind behind them for extra speed.

It was only four in the afternoon with Delhi only twenty minutes away.

She spun the helm and the steering rotors twisted, forcing the prow of the *Beauty* through a rapid one-hundred-and-twenty-degree turn. She whistled Remy again.

"*Mon dieu*, Madame Captain, I almost spilled my cognac."

"*Monsieur* Darras, we are twenty minutes from Delhi. I require the best exertion of your art."

"You wish me to vent hot air such that we descend in a smooth line and touchdown exactly as we reach Delhi?"

"We are of a mind, *Monsieur* Darras."

"Very good, Captain, it will be as you desire."

The smooth descent went as planned. Remy Darras might be a terrible liar but his skill in managing the ship's buoyancy was undeniable. The landscape dropped away beneath them as they descended from the high plateau into the wide fertile lands that ran the length of the foothills below the Himalayas.

Ahead of them ragged streams of chimney smoke streamed away east across the city. The sun hung mid-way down the western sky, casting shadows that accentuated the tall central buildings.

Ding had gone up to the open deck. The communication tube from the lookout post whistled. Qi lifted it from its socket and pressed it to her ear

"*Jackanape* sighted," Ding shouted above the wind noise. "Forty-five degrees to starboard."

The angle was too great for her to see without leaving her post. She moved the end of the tube to her mouth. "How far?"

"We arrive before them," came his reply.

They were about five miles out when the air-dock became visible: a rectangular field of close-cropped grass dotted with groups of buildings. The ice warehouses were in the northeast corner, and a group of Bainbridge ships were docked around their own storage buildings. A couple of independent ice buckets were docked near the general trade warehouses; there was no activity, which meant the workers could start unloading as soon as *Beauty* made dock.

Qi did not expect the perfection Remy had promised, but he was close. They were at two hundred feet by the altimeter and half a mile out when she disengaged the power to the main propeller and their forward velocity dropped. The easterly wind kept pushing the ship off course. Qi adjusted the thrusters to compensate for the drift and keep their heading true.

A team of five dock workers emerged from the customs building and grouped around a mooring pier close to the other landed ships. Qi adjusted her course and the four thruster power levers. The *Beauty* drifted smoothly into position. But it wasn't the ship's speed that was the problem: it was the tonnage of ice in the hold. Misjudge the approach and the *Beauty* would be smashed to pieces as the cargo met the brick building. The sooner she could get *Beauty* on the ground the better.

She saw the forward lines drop down, thrown out by Ding and Ichiro. She was now so close all she could see was the pier. The two forward lines went taut as the workers below caught hold. She reduced power further until the thrusters were just compensating for the wind. Up on top deck she knew Remy would be closing off the valves that allowed the super-heated steam from the boilers into the array of pipes that ran up into the balloon envelopes.

The *Beauty* came to a halt a couple of yards from the mooring pier. The pier seemed to be rising as the ship sank to the ground. The head of a man came into view followed by the rest of him, like a ship coming over the horizon: an Indian in dungarees, the uniform of the dockers.

There was a gentle jolt as the ship settled onto the grass. Qi cut the power to the thrusters and stepped away. She turned to Otto who had his hand on a large red button set into the wall. "Give them a blast, Otto."

He grinned. "*Ja*, Captain." He pushed the palm of his hand against the button and a klaxon roared, filling the ship. She glanced at the chronometer, which ticked five seconds.

"Again." The noise blasted out

Another five seconds. "Once more." He pressed the button and the klaxon roared again. Qi stepped across to a lever and gripped it with both hands. The final five seconds passed and she threw the switch that disengaged the Faraday device.

Even though she was ready for it, she staggered as the weight of every object on board ship—and the vessel itself—quadrupled and it sank into the ground.

The crew of the *Beauty* had done this dozens of times. In the engine room Ding and Ichiro would be banking the fires in the furnace; on deck Remy would be releasing the steam pressure and ensuring the balloons deflated neatly and without burning on the pipework. Qi, accompanied by Otto, made her way through into the cargo hold. The lights were already burning and she could hear the Australian cook, Terry Montgomery, hammering at the frozen bolts of the main hatch.

She had found Terry in a Buddhist monastery in China. She had never asked why he had been there. He seemed to think her arrival had been some sort of sign; he had immediately attached himself to her. He had a lean strength but she had never seen him raise his hand in anger to anyone. Right now he was exerting that strength on a particularly reluctant bolt.

She stood back to give him and Otto space to free the ramp. Otto grabbed the wooden handle of the winch and wound it down.

The hot air of the Delhi evening flooded in and did battle with the frozen atmosphere inside the hold, forming a low mist that flowed along the icy deck. The dock workers lounged in a casual group a few yards away, waiting instead of rushing forward to start unloading.

The reason was clear. Like a tiger ready to pounce, Walter Templeton, Constable of His Majesty's Customs and Excise, stood poised with a polished clip-board in one hand.

Qi resisted the temptation to glance into the back of the cargo hold. Instead she walked steadily down the ramp forcing a smile on to her face.

"Constable Templeton, this is a surprise."

4

"Captain Qi."

Templeton strode up the deck. He loomed over her, blocking the light.

"Is this really necessary?" she asked as he stepped past her into the aisle. One could hope he might slip and maybe break his neck (or at least break something important), but he was experienced at walking the ice decks.

Ding had disembarked on the outside and now stood on the grass, glaring at Templeton. He glanced at Qi, who shrugged. There was nothing they could do.

"Would it be possible to unload the cargo you've inspected?"

"No."

Templeton wandered up the aisle at a slow pace, examining the straps and looking above and below the ice blocks. What did he think he was looking for? Anything under the ice would get crushed.

Qi looked back at Ding; she jerked her head towards the back of the hold. Ding started up the ramp.

"Please keep your crew out of the hold while I make my inspection." She turned round and saw Templeton frowning at her. She waved Ding back and he descended again.

"Hey! English!"

Both Templeton and Qi turned at the sound coming from above them. Remy Darras stood at the gantry entrance.

Templeton turned his head to Qi. "I believe I asked you to keep your crew out of the cargo hold."

"*Monsieur* Darras, I would appreciate it if you would leave the deck."

"But I am not on the deck. I am not interfering with this stupid English."

"You will kindly treat me with some respect," Templeton said in a tone that would brook no argument from a sane person.

"And why would I do that, English?" Darras's taunting voice echoed around the cargo hold, along with the occasional crack of warming ice and what, to Qi at least, sounded like footsteps. She moved towards Templeton, whose attention was thoroughly occupied with the Frenchman.

"Because, Monsieur," countered Templeton. "I can have you locked up."

"I am not one of your British citizens; there is nothing you can do."

"Or I can make Captain Qi wait here without unloading until all your precious cargo is melted into worthlessness."

The Frenchman stepped forward and placed his ungloved hands on the icy rail. He took a deep breath.

"*Allons enfants de la patrie*," sang Darras. "*Le jour de gloire est arrivé / Le jour de gloire est arrivé /—*" With each refrain his voice grew louder. Templeton tried to speak but his voice was completely drowned out by the French national anthem.

Qi watched Darras's eyes, and saw a flick above and behind them. She crossed behind Templeton to ensure he did not take his eyes off Darras and then called up.

"Remy?"

Darras broke off his song. "*Oui*, Captain?"

"Why don't you take Otto to a bar and get drunk?"

"*Bien sur*, that is an excellent *ideé*." He peeled his palms carefully from the freezing steel of the rail and went back into the ship.

She faced Templeton. "I apologise, Constable. I do not think *Monsieur* Darras subscribes to the *Entente Cordiale* between your two countries. And he does not appreciate the hard work you do. I will be sure to censure him about his behaviour." She conjured up the most pleasant and innocent smile she could. "Why don't I leave you to finish your inspection? Perhaps you would like a hot mug of tea?"

After the abuse from Darras, the earnestness of her tone confused him and he accepted her offer.

She strode away across the deck and broke into a run as soon as she was out on the grass. Hand over hand she climbed one of the ladders attached to the outside of the ship up to the afterdeck, where Ding held the dripping box he had recovered from the hold while Templeton had his attention on Darras—who stood nearby, grinning like a madman.

"You could have made it worse, Remy," she said.

"We have recovered the item and we are safe, *non*?"

She sighed, there was no point arguing. She had been careless and they had been right.

"Why?" asked Ding.

She shrugged. Why indeed. Inspections were not unknown but they were rare. If it had been serious, Templeton would have had a platoon of soldiers to search the whole ship and he wouldn't have been so lax about keeping the crew out of the hold. He would have had them all in one place under guard before he started the inspection.

It stank.

She leaned on the rail and looked up. If the *Jackanape* made it to port before Templeton finished, all their fancy flying would be wasted and their cargo would spend a warm night melting.

*　*　*

The *Jackanape* was on its final approach when Templeton declared that he was satisfied. The other ship was still twenty minutes from touchdown; being hydrogen-based it did not have the ability to land quickly like the *Beauty*.

Templeton handed the half-frozen mug of tea to Qi as he signed off the report and passed her a copy. She glanced at it and gave him another smile. "Thank you."

He nodded and walked towards the administration building.

"We can unload now?" she called after him.

He did not turn or answer but raised his hand to the lounging workers. At his gesture towards the *Beauty*, they climbed to their feet. Qi climbed up to the walkway to watch as they went smoothly to work moving the ice from the hold. None too soon: even the ice on the gantry was melting.

Ding came through the upper door and handed her a backpack containing a single heavy item.

"What about the others?"

"Gone."

"All right, you stay on board. I'll see what I can get for this."

He reached out and laid his hand gently on her shoulder. "Be careful," he said in Mandarin.

"I will."

The sun was dipping low as she walked down the ramp beside the dock workers, who were using ropes and pulleys to manhandle another ice block onto the steam-powered truck that chugged just inside the hold. They'd be at it for another few hours.

She took a circuitous route away from the administration block and down towards the main passenger buildings. There were a couple of small British vessels in dock as well as a zeppelin. The big ships did not come to Delhi; they went via Bombay and then down the coast to Ceylon. Only the smaller lines plied the route across the top the country, from Bombay across to Calcutta via Delhi, along the base of the mountains.

On the street she hailed a rickshaw and headed into the city.

5

The streets of Delhi sweated in the dying light of the day and the sky took on a purple hue. The low sun's half-light made the shadows thick as night.

The rickshaw driver flew through the streets that bustled with people on foot, horses, bicycles; there were carts pulled by oxen and goats, and a variety of mechanicals from personal carriages to big huffing omnibuses overflowing with passengers. Her driver gave not so much as a sideways glance as they passed a fruit vendor and an engineer engaged in a screaming argument beside a toppled cart half-crushed by a steam carriage.

From the wide and tarmacadamed road that led from the air-dock to the city, the driver turned off on to narrower streets. They passed markets where their speed dropped to almost nothing while the driver shouted at the pedestrians, and trotted along side streets splattering effluent against the walls and onto anyone who had the misfortune to be standing nearby.

Finally they reached a stand of small shops built in the typical British style that pervaded the larger Indian cities. The driver stopped in the middle of the street and Qi dismounted, clutching the box. She took a few coins from her belt and passed them over. Flashing a grin, he headed off.

Someone had thoughtfully constructed a walkway to keep pedestrian feet out of the mire that comprised the street, but she still had to step carefully to reach it. It had been such a long time since she had worn women's attire, and she was not sure she possessed any. Skirts were impractical aboard ship, bound as they were to get caught on the metal work, and when worn visiting a city they would only attract dirt. Dock worker's boots and sturdy trousers were the order of the day.

Qi knew her clothing was unusual. She was used to being stared at and even mistaken for a man on occasion. Looking feminine was not something she considered necessary in her line of work, and she had never encountered any occasion when it was required. Nor did she comment on the choices of others: live and let live was her motto.

But the Caucasian lad with the badly trimmed black hair under a cloth cap—lounging against a brick wall outside the shop she intended to enter—caught her attention. He wore a light jacket over a loose shirt with trousers and practical boots, in his mouth was a short clay pipe, and he was casually sharpening a knife on a whetstone. Despite all that, the boy looked distinctly female with his soft features and, if Qi was not much mistaken, breasts: not prominent, but there nonetheless.

Qi realised first that she was staring, and then that she had stopped walking. She nodded at the boy, as if they were slightly acquainted, and received a smile and nod in return.

She pushed open the shop door. It had no signage, but she knew this was the right place. The dark interior held a wide selection of items for sale. There was no organisation, and no consistency: a bicycle, a lady's reticule, some golf clubs. One pile consisted of bits of machinery even she did not recognise. The smaller items were displayed on pieces of furniture which were themselves for sale. Most were in reasonable condition, but everything was coated in a layer of dust.

"Captain Qi."

From the back of the shop emerged Emily Wong, wearing a cheongsam that may have fitted her once but was now several sizes too large, as if she had shrunk. Her age was indeterminate, but in excess of a hundred if her wrinkles were counted like rings in a tree trunk. Her pure white hair was tied back in a thick braid.

"Emily."

There were no pleasantries to be spoken. Qi had known Emily since she first travelled with her father on the *Beauty*. Emily had always looked the same, and she existed for only one reason. Qi lifted the box, expecting Emily to invite her into the back to examine the item.

But she did not. Instead she stood impassively in the half-light.

Something moved behind her. Someone. Kuan-Yin Sun's portly frame emerged from the gloom. With his high-quality silk kimono, leather sandals, long, drooping moustache, and conical hat, he looked every inch the Mandarin he pretended to be. There were other figures behind him in the dark: his bully boys, no doubt.

"I am disappointed, Qi." He spoke in Mandarin though she knew he had an excellent command of English. His voice was very light in tone, so unlike the weight of his character and business.

"I am sorry I did not call on you first. We were delayed by the port authorities."

"Indeed you were." Kuan-Yin stepped further into the light. His face was smiling though there was little mirth in his eyes. "You did not bring your cargo to me on your last trip. It seems that was not your intention this time, either."

Qi glanced behind herself. There were two more Chinese in suits a size too small outside on the street. If she couldn't talk her way out of this one, it could end up being quite painful for someone. She hoped it would not be her.

"I did not know I was required to sell through you, Sun." She took a step back. "I can get a better price selling through Emily, here."

His humourless smile broadened to reveal an expanse of teeth with gaps. "Emily is not buying from you anymore."

"Isn't that up to her?"

Kuan-Yin did not respond. Qi already knew the answer; it would not be hard for him to ensure she had nowhere to sell smuggled goods.

"There are other cities."

The grin did not leave his face. "I wonder," he said, picking some imagined piece of food from between his teeth. "How will you travel to those cities without a vessel?"

"You wouldn't destroy my *Beauty*."

"I do not need to destroy her, Qi. Merely repossess her."

Her heart sank because she knew it was true. She might love the *Frozen Beauty* but she did not own her—or, at least, she could not prove she did. It was a fact she chose to ignore. She had lived on board any time she had not been at Catholic school. Her father had been the captain before she took over, and while she might not have a piece of paper that proved she owned her, she loved the ship with all her heart.

And no one would take *Beauty* from her.

She lifted a curiously shaped iron paperweight from the desk beside her and weighed it in her hand as she eyed Kuan-Yin. The smile slipped from his face. She flung it with all her force at the light fitting above his head, shattering the glass.

Turning, she threw herself towards the front door. The two heavies could not see into the shop, but they anticipated Qi fleeing the premises. The nearest one lunged at her as she came through the door. She twisted out of his way and, as he flew past, gave him a push that sent him through the plate glass with a crash of glass and blood.

She turned to face the second but he was not attacking. His attention was riveted on the knife at his throat. The boy-girl had him pinned but did not press her fatal advantage. Qi did not hesitate. She slammed her fist into his solar plexus. He went down with blood trickling from a cut in his neck. Qi looked at the boy-girl, who smiled and shrugged.

"Fanning, ma'am," he said and held out his hand. As Qi shook it, she noted the grip was firm but the skin was soft.

"Qi Zang."

"Reckoned there'd be trouble when those two showed up." There was a growl and shout from the shop. "Shall we be going?"

The boy took off like lightning dancing across the walkway. Qi hesitated but a moment, then set off after him.

6

It was late evening when Qi, with Fanning tagging along, reached the Cold Heart: a traditional Irish pub run by one Jacob O'Donnell, relocated to one of the slums of Delhi. More precisely, O'Donnell claimed it was traditional; Qi had never even travelled as far as Persia, let alone Europe, so she took his word.

She pushed through crowd of sailors and nodded to the ones she knew. The crew of the *Jackanape* did not seem to be here. The air was thick with smoke from cigarettes and pipes and filled with the noise of a hundred conversations, from clandestine whispers to raucous laughs. And the smell. Not something one could even begin to describe.

There was a break in the crowd as she moved forward and she spotted the rest of her crew seated round a table towards the rear. Qi tried to squeeze past Ichiro's muscled back. He stood and bowed to her; Terry and Remy grabbed their drinks as he knocked the table. Qi was still unable to get past. Laying her hand on his arm so he looked up at her, she gestured for him to move and he stepped to the side.

Ding, on a bench seat against the wall, pushed up against Terry Montgomery. The moustachioed Australian managed to find some room against the dandy Frenchman. Qi sat, her leg pressing against Ding's, her perch precarious on the end of the unpadded wooden bench.

Fanning leaned back against the wall next to her and pulled out his pipe. In that position, the non-male appearance of his chest was even more obvious. Qi stared for a moment then shook her head. She saw Otto, Remy, and Terry staring as Fanning struck a match and took a pull on the pipe, which smoked satisfactorily.

"This is Fanning," she said by way of explanation. "He helped me earlier today."

Three sets of eyes, set into confused frowns, focused on her at the word he. She shrugged; a discussion of Fanning's apparent gender did not seem polite with him standing there.

She was still holding the box with the smuggled item. It was not something she could hide. Ichiro broke the silence in the only way he could; he reached out with his coal-grimed fingers and touched the box lightly, then turned his hand so the palm was uppermost and put his head on one side with a querying expression.

Captain Qi sighed. She took Ichiro's hand, hers only a fraction the size of his, and folded his fingers in her palm. She shook her head.

"Problem, Captain?" asked Ding.

"Nothing I can't handle."

"Kuan-Yin Sun?"

She nodded. "We just need to find another buyer."

Terry Montgomery took a drink from his pint mug. "Why don't you just sell through him, Captain?"

"He is a criminal, *Herr* Montgomery," said Otto. "We should not do business with him."

Montgomery responded in a quiet but insistent voice. "And we're smugglers, Mr von Krone. And, in case you were unaware, that makes us criminals."

"He is more bad."

Qi put the palm of her hand down flat on the table and the bickering ceased. "I am the one who is smuggling. If anyone is a criminal, it's me and me alone. You do not know anything about it."

"I dislike to bring up the subject, *Capitaine*, but our wages are due."

"You'll get your share from the sale of the cargo tomorrow, Monsieur Darras."

"But it will not be enough if you cannot dispose of all of the cargo." He nodded at the box.

"You'll get everything you're due."

* * *

Ding walked beside Qi as they headed back to the ship through dark streets lit by the occasional electric streetlamp. The air was dense with heat and moisture. Qi glanced back and saw Fanning still following a few paces behind like an obedient dog. An obedient dog smoking a pipe. Qi stopped in a puddle of light and turned. Fanning could only be seen as an outline.

"Something I can do for you, Fanning?"

"No, ma'am," he replied. "But maybe there's something we can do for each other, if I might be so bold as to suggest a course of action."

"What do you have in mind?"

"I have a yearning for travel, Captain. I am a long way from home." Fanning stood comfortably, feet apart, relaxed as if he had not a care in the world.

"If I pay my crew I will have no money for fuel. If I do not pay them I will not have a crew. The *Beauty* isn't going anywhere, so I don't think I can help you."

Fanning took a step forward. In the light, his features looked even more feminine than usual. "And if I were to provide you with an alternative purchaser for your little trinket? Would that gain me passage aboard your fine vessel?"

"If you were willing to work, then I believe the answer to that would be yes."

"Then let us find somewhere where we can talk privately."

7

The captain and Fanning headed back to the ship. Ding watched them moving away, passing in and out of the glowing yellow pools from the streetlights. The night was not quiet; here near the docks there was always something happening. A heavy steam tractor puffed by pulling a train of three trucks, on its way to the air-dock. A street walker called to him hopefully from the other side of the street. He shook his head, that was not a comfort he needed, and she drifted away into the night.

It was possible for a person to walk the streets alone and be unmolested among the pick-pockets, street gangs and others who made their living in the dark—if they knew their business. Ding leaned back against the wall and pulled a clay pipe from inside his jacket, along with a tobacco pouch and matches. Smoking was the one pleasure he allowed himself, and then only when he wasn't looking out for Qi.

He had been first mate aboard the *Beauty* for all of Qi's captaincy, and her father's before that. Fifteen years, perhaps, since they began their life of semi-piracy on behalf of the Tiandihui clan. They had never stolen from another ship, and had killed only when there was no other choice. He was content enough with their record.

He held the leather pouch open with one hand and dipped the pipe inside, gently packing the moist tobacco into the bowl until it was almost full. This was a good night to let the fumes fill his mind and relax him. With the pouch back in his pocket, he placed the pipe in his mouth and struck a match.

The flaring light illuminated the outlines of a man's face; he stood a short distance away, looking back at Ding.

The first mate did not react, but raised the match to the bowl and sucked the air through, dragging the flame down onto the weed. The flame flared back at each puff, lighting the face that still watched him. The tobacco smouldered. Ding shook the match to extinguish the light and flung it to the ground.

"Can I help you, Kuan-Yin Sun?" he said in Mandarin.

"Your captain has forgotten herself, Dingbang Hsieh."

Ding levered himself from the wall and stood facing the shadow. He gave a bow that was just the right side of respectful but made it clear he did not think the recipient deserved the honour. "She was never your servant, Sun."

"She inherited the vessel, she inherits the debt."

"She is a spirit of the air. She will not be contained."

Kuan-Yin Sun stepped forward, bringing his wide frame into the light, while in the dark behind him three hulking bodyguards made their presence known.

"We have known each other a long time, Dingbang," he said. "I don't need to tell you what the family will do to her if she fails to keep up the payments."

Ding was well aware how much the 'family' cared for people. Anyone who broke the rules met their ancestors too early. Sun watched him as if he could read the thoughts that played through his mind.

"You need to persuade her, Dingbang," he continued. "She will listen to you. You have her father's authority."

"Only her father had that."

There was the sudden sound of heavy feet, iron boot-nails clicking on flagstones. More than one set of feet, more than one person not afraid of the dark, heading in their direction. Both of them glanced towards the sound. Two uniformed police and another in the garb of a customs agent marched through the light of a lamp, heading in their direction.

Sun backed into the shadow once more. "Listen to my words, Dingbang Hsieh. Captain Qi cannot fly, and she cannot sell the goods she has. I own this city. Prevail upon her, my friend; make her see sense and she will once more be able to fly in the ship that she loves so much."

And he was gone, as the thudding of boots on stone grew closer.

The British were not afraid to be seen in the light and stopped in front of Ding. He bowed his head with the respect one gives to an unfriendly dog when one is unsure of its intentions.

"You're the mate from the *Frozen Beauty*."

Ding did not acknowledge the recognition, but he did not deny it. Constable Templeton and he were acquainted.

"Who was that you were talking to?"

"He is a Chinaman like myself."

"It was Kuan-Yin Sun."

Ding took a long pull at his pipe and allowed the smoke to tickle his throat before letting it out gently.

"What did he want?"

"He wanted to know when my captain intended to take the ship out again."

"Did he now?"

Templeton glanced in the direction Sun had headed. "I wonder what he's up to."

Ding found it convenient to ignore rhetorical statements, particularly those that came from people with authority. Templeton returned his attention to Ding.

"What did you tell him?"

"My captain is an air spirit."

Templeton hesitated and then harrumphed. Ding suspected he had not a single whit of poetry in his heart. Possibly he had no heart at all.

"All right, well, you better get along."

Ding had met many men like Templeton, not just British but of all nations: men who felt they must control, because if they did not, then somehow they were the victim. They were easy to deal with; one simply did as they wanted. As long as they were in sight.

Ding nodded his head once more and headed off in the direction of the air-dock while Templeton and his associates turned away to follow Sun's trail. Sun would be long gone by now, and they would never find where he had gone. Of that much Ding was certain.

The sun had barely broached the horizon and all the city streets were still in shadow. The air was the coolest it would be for this day, and almost refreshing—save for the stink of the effluent that ran through the open sewers.

Fanning led the way through the back streets, between buildings that seemed to fold in over Qi and her. Balconies protruded in haphazard patterns; women and children leaned out over the railings and called across to neighbours.

Behind Fanning walked the captain. They had come to an agreement: if Fanning could get a buyer for the package, Qi would let Fanning take passage on the *Beauty*—as long as she was willing to work. It was a good deal as far as Fanning was concerned. She was tired of Delhi, and the lack of any enquiry as to her gender status, even in private, showed the captain to be a person of good manners.

They had talked until the early hours when Ding had come in and related his encounters.

As the sky had turned pink with the dawn they had made their way through the shadows of the air-docks. The captain had taken a complicated route with the intention of evading both criminals and customs.

Fanning retraced the steps she had taken the previous day when pawning the woman's jewellery. As they travelled, the buildings around them changed from tenements to warehouses and factories. They passed over a river flowing through the city and under the tube railway elevated on brickwork arches that spanned the flowing water. On each bank, at opposite ends of the span, stood the pumping stations pushing pressurised air into the tubes.

They reached the far side of the river and climbed the slope into a pleasanter region of the city. The roads became wider and cleaner, with sewer pipes below the surface. The buildings were more solid, more ornate; their glass-filled windows were wider.

At this time of the morning there were few people on the streets, and those were involved in commerce of one sort or another. They did not judge her looks any more than Qi's Chinese features because they themselves were just as varied.

The door to the pawn shop was locked tight when they arrived, but Fanning was not put off. They circled round to the end of the shops, passed down an alley wide enough for a cart, and made their way to the rear of the building.

A young Chinese woman was brushing dust from the red-tiled steps onto the bricks which had been laid in a herringbone pattern at the rear. Low walls separated each of the shops' yards, and there were double-width doors for loading at the back of each building. Three shops down, a large cart stood close against the building and boxes of fruit were being taken inside.

The girl ceased brushing and eyed them suspiciously.

Fanning approached her and gave her a smile guaranteed to win the heart of any woman. "Is your master in, pretty one?"

She paused a moment to regard Fanning's features, then turned her head towards the darkness beyond and shouted some words in Mandarin. Fanning glanced at Qi, who shrugged.

There was a wait. The girl continued to study Fanning, but hers wasn't the face of someone enamoured: more the look of someone trying to recall a word for a crossword clue. Fanning took a step back as a robed figure emerged from the darkness beyond the door.

In the daylight, Fanning saw that the robe she had assumed was black was a very dark green, and of cotton rather than silk. The shop-owner took in Fanning, his eyes sliding across her features without comment and then moving to Qi in her aviator's clothes. His eyes returned to Fanning.

"Is this Mrs Devonshire?"

"You might say this is another Mrs Devonshire, sir."

His eyes narrowed. "I do not think I am in business for this Mrs Devonshire."

"You have not seen what she has to offer." Fanning gestured to Qi, who stepped forward and lifted the box.

The man took a step back as if he'd been threatened with a knife and raised his hand to defend himself. "I am not in business for Captain Qi."

"You have not even seen what she has to offer."

"It does not matter. I do not wish to buy," he said quickly. "I would not want it even if it were free."

"Someone been talking to you?" asked Fanning.

The Chinaman made no comment.

"Someone been threatening you?"

At that moment a police whistle shrieked. As one they turned. Across the low walls Fanning saw the policeman blowing hard on his whistle to summon assistance.

Fanning looked back at the building but both the Chinaman and the girl were gone, having disappeared into the black interior.

"Let's go!" shouted Fanning and took off down the back alley. Qi was taller; she took more time to get into motion but Fanning could hear her footsteps as she loped along behind.

Fanning placed her feet as carefully as she could manage, as they charged down the cobbled path. Cobblestones could be so treacherous. She glanced ahead. Faces peered out from the shops and upper windows but no one shouted. The whistle sounded intermittently from behind them; the policeman was undoubtedly in pursuit, trying to blow the whistle while he ran.

Fanning spotted a tiny alley to the right and took it. The more corners they could put between themselves and the police, the better. The alley passed under the building and then out again. It emptied into some kind of scrap-metal yard where their way was barred by a tall gate with a padlock. Fanning threw herself at it and made it halfway up. She climbed fast, fell over the top and landed on the other side.

Qi couldn't climb holding the box, and behind her the policeman had reached the far end of the alley.

"Throw it," shouted Fanning. Qi hesitated for only a moment, judged the distance, and tossed the box. Without further hesitation she began to climb. Fanning watched the box arc over the gate and grabbed it with a smooth swinging motion.

Once the box was safe, Fanning leapt away through the maze of piled and rusting metal. She heard the soft thud of Qi's feet landing and the shrill blasts of the policeman's whistle muffled by the covered alley. Moments later they reached the edge of the river. They slowed and Fanning looked both ways. The bridge they had used before was closest, but she turned away from it and headed in the other direction with Captain Qi at her side.

9

Sunlight broke into a million shards across the surface of the river. Boats crisscrossed its surface: sailing ships large and small, fishing boats, family boats, steamers, and ferry boats. And in the heart of the river sat the unbalanced monstrosity of *HMS Kilimanjaro*—a ship that was obsolete before she was completed: A water-borne vessel with a Faraday device at her heart. The warship, bristling with artillery, floated as high in the water as one of the ferry boats that steamed past her a dozen times a day. Her stacks churned out smoke and steam all day and night. If her Faraday device failed for even the shortest time she would sink into the mud of the river, never to be recovered.

At first glance the *Kilimanjaro* looked like an ordinary Royal Navy battleship, only much bigger, with a complement of nearly two thousand men. But this was a ship that could navigate any river that was wide enough with almost no regard to its depth. She had been commissioned to support British foreign policy: when the Servants of the Crown didn't like the way a small government was behaving they would send in the gunboats. But, by the time the *Kilimanjaro* had been completed, the Royal Navy was almost exclusively air- and void-borne. So here she stayed, watching over the capital of India, a slumbering monster that could fire on any opponent within twenty miles. No one knew, save perhaps her crew, whether she was capable of movement along the river any more.

Fanning led the way along the riverside as the sun steadily mounted in the sky and the heat became almost intolerable.

"Where are we going, Fanning?"

"Somewhere I know, we'll be safe there. You can plan your next move."

Next move? thought Qi. All she had to do was give the box to Kuan-Yin Sun; he would pay her enough to get them back into the mountains for the next cargo of ice. It was that simple. But her heart rebelled. Why should she? The *Beauty* was hers.

They reached a point where a tributary flowed down into the river from a residential area of the city, a natural stinking sewer. A rough bridge of planks led into a low area that looked as if it regularly flooded; it was covered with a treacherously green swathe of grass. Something to welcome the unwary before it swallowed them up in its muddy grip. Another plank bridge led along the tributary's bank toward the houses.

Fanning crossed the bridge.

The captain's leather costume chafed as she sweated in the heat. She needed a drink. Tea would do if something stronger couldn't be found. Alcohol was not as easy to get hold of as she might like in India. One had to make compromises.

Fanning was across the planks in a moment; his light frame barely moved the slotted wood. But it certainly gave when Qi put her booted foot on it. She edged across it almost laughing at herself. She had climbed the *Beauty*'s balloon rigging in a storm to tie down a broken line when there was nothing between her and a drop of hundreds of feet to a stony death. But this was different, she told herself. The stinking unpleasantness of the water was a much nastier threat.

On the other side she had to extend her step to catch up. "Is it much further?"

Fanning did not answer but pointed at a ramshackle pile of wood and stone that barely qualified as a building, squatting on a slight rise near a bend in the river.

As they approached, the broken building resolved itself into several distinct hovels sitting within the collapsed walls and remains of what might have been an old fort constructed to defend the bend in the river. Stone steps went down to the river's edge. The whole area was paved in stone underneath the coarse grass and bushes.

There was the smell of cooking, and thin lines of smoke rose from small fires. They saw no one. Fanning stopped in the middle of the open area surrounded by the shacks.

"Guru Parnashri?"

There was movement all around them as women emerged from hiding. Qi frowned and stared. They were wearing saris but most of them did not look like women; they were men. Now she knew who they were. These were *hijra*. She had seen them on the streets occasionally, some begging and some selling themselves.

One came out and sat facing them. Fanning greeted her, pressing his palms together and bowing his head. "*Namaste*, Guru Parnashri."

"*Namaste*, Liza Fanning." The guru nodded. "Who is your aviator friend?"

"Captain Qi, who has promised to take me away if I help her."

"Captain Qi, *namaste*." She nodded again and Qi returned the gesture. "Do you tire of our company, Liza Fanning?"

Liza? That removed Qi's remaining doubt. A girl who dressed as a man, among men who dressed as women. It had a certain balance. Then Qi smiled inwardly, considering what she herself wore, what she considered normal clothing; she too was a woman dressed as a man.

A timid *hijra* wearing a red-patterned sari, tattered round the hem, came up to them and touched Fanning on the arm. He passed Fanning an envelope.

"Will you eat with us, Captain Qi?" said the guru. "And perhaps you would like to tell us your problems. It may be we can help."

It would be the height of bad manners to reject the offer, and it seemed they were safe for now. Fanning was reading the letter he— no, she'd removed from the envelope.

Qi sat down next to Fanning, "Thank you." She was curious about the letter but felt it impolite to ask.

The guru nodded to one of the others. Qi looked round and noticed two *hijra* busying themselves around a fire. The remainder simply sat round them and watched in silence. It was a little unnerving.

The food was served up on wooden plates: a small amount of rice and some vegetables, along with a piece of fish. The guru and Fanning ate with their fingers, using their right hands only, but she had been given chopsticks. She could barely remember the last time she had eaten using them; they used metal cutlery on the *Beauty*, and these were older than chopsticks had a right to be. She could not refuse to use them, as the guru had tried to make her feel at home, but she did wonder how clean they were.

They made the meal last though there was little enough of it. To finish there was a thin tea that was barely more than water, but it had been boiled. She had seen them spooning it from the bubbling pot. It was surprisingly refreshing. When they had finished, the same *hijra* who had prepared the meal whisked away the plates.

Guru Parnashri turned her brown eyes on Qi. "Captain Qi, what is your problem?"

10

They took their leave of the strange community when the greatest heat of the day had passed. Not that the small group of lean-tos provided much protection. The company had been friendly enough. One of the *hijra* waved a handkerchief as Qi departed and wiped a tear from his eye.

"Would you be willing to carry a passenger, Captain?" asked Fanning.

"Did we not discuss it?"

"This would be Mrs Cameron, not me," said Fanning. "She's one of my clients. I sell things for her."

"Is she wanted?"

"Oh no, she's straight as a die. Proper English lady, but with a husband who ain't worth a spit." Fanning took out the letter and passed it to her. "Seems he's noticed she's been selling her jewellery to pay for his gambling."

Qi unfolded the letter. The handwriting was refined and clear with delicate curves, perfect except where it had been blotted by a drop of water—or, perhaps, a tear. The thrust of the letter was simple enough. Without saying so precisely, she indicated her husband had become violent and she would like to follow up on Fanning's offer of escape.

"You offered her passage on my ship?" Qi did not like people who took advantage.

"Oh no, Captain, I assure you I offered her an escape before I even met you. But if there were any way she could be accommodated, I'm sure she would be grateful."

"I am not a charity for waifs and strays, Fanning. I have more pressing issues, like making sure I keep my ship."

But even as she said it, she had the beginnings of an idea.

*   *   *

Having sent Fanning off on errands, Qi took a roundabout route back towards the air-docks, making sure she passed through an area heavily populated by Chinese. Having ensured she was seen, she headed for a pub near the docks, too far from them to be frequented by customs men but close enough for her to hear the gossip. The bartender was an ex-flyer who had lost a leg and an arm in a crash years before.

"Nice to see you in here, Captain Qi," he said. "First drink on the house for any captain. What'll you have?"

"Gin rickey, Mac."

"Got no ice."

She smiled. "I get enough ice."

He took down a glass and gave it a wipe with a clean cloth before pouring in a short measure and adding the lime from a dusty bottle. He pushed it across the bar. She took a sip. The gin was rough but the lime and soda smoothed it out.

"*Jackanape* cleared, Mac?" she asked.

"Aye, this morning, but the *Blossom* came over earlier."

She nodded. "Yes, they were a day behind us."

"Shouldn't you be lifting? Hanging about for any reason?"

She knew he knew why, but he had the decency not to mention it. "Few things to sort out," she replied taking another swig.

The door slammed open. Qi looked in the mirror behind the bar as light flooded in. Two Indians with more muscle than fat, and they had plenty of that, moved into the room.

They scanned it for trouble as Kuan-Yin Sun sauntered in, now wearing a grey suit that was tailored to a perfect fit. He looked suave enough to be a businessman. He pulled off his white gloves.

He looked at her and a cold smile spread across his face. "Captain Qi, so fortuitous that we have bumped into one another."

"How did you know I was here?"

"You should be careful who you associate with; not everyone is as trustworthy as I am."

"You would sell your mother for a wen."

She turned away from him and took a careful sip. Sun covered the distance between them, his shoes slapping across the stone floor. He became a close and intrusive presence at her side.

"The time has come to pay up, Captain Qi," he said into her ear. "Or forfeit the *Beauty*."

"Something smells rotten in here, Mac."

The bartender grinned. Sun moved back slightly and snapped his fingers. In the mirror Qi observed one of Sun's enforcers closing in on her. She turned at the last moment and flung what remained of her drink into his face. He flung his hands up too late; the lime went into his eyes.

Taking advantage of his blindness, she planted her knee where it would have the greatest effect. He went down with a whine. The second bodyguard was on her in a moment trying to get her in a bear hug. As she smelled his sweat she pulled his knife from its sheath and pressed the point into his stomach. Not enough to penetrate far, but enough to make him notice.

He jerked away.

Qi heard the unmistakable click of a gun being cocked. She looked to her right, straight into the barrel of Kuan-Yin Sun's revolver.

Behind him, Mac had picked up a bottle and was ready to swipe it across Sun's head. She shook her head slightly. Mac frowned, but after a pause he lowered it. For one thing, she did not want Mac pulled into trouble that might leave him with even fewer limbs than he now possessed. On a more personal note, the blow to the head might make Sun pull the trigger.

"Really, Captain Qi, is that any way to behave? You are outnumbered and quite alone."

She turned back to the bar. Mac made her a new drink; she pulled out a coin and tossed it on the bar in exchange.

"What do you want, Sun?" she said, swallowing the entire glassful in one gulp.

"Do not play games. Deliver the item and we will discuss how we may keep you flying."

"Indebted to you."

"More indebted," he said. "But not to me, to the family."

"I don't suppose you'd consider a bribe." She turned to face him, and leaned casually on the bar.

The grin returned to his face. "There is nothing you could offer that would tempt me." And the grin disappeared. "Enough of this time wasting. I want the item and I want it now. If you do not supply it, I will kill your crew one at a time. Who shall it be first? Dingbang, perhaps?"

She slumped. "All right. It's been given to someone for safekeeping."

"Lead the way, Captain."

Qi walked towards the door. The enforcer on the floor climbed cautiously to his feet and scowled at her. She glanced into the corner, where Terry Montgomery had been watching the proceedings from behind a newspaper. The cook caught her brief gesture, a move that would have been meaningless to anyone who had not shipped with someone who could only communicate through sign-language.

She stepped out into the hot, sweaty daylight with Sun at her back, the gun hidden but still trained on her.

11

Fanning approached the *Cherry Blossom in Winter* as the ground crew manhandled blocks and sheets of ice out of the hold and onto the waiting steamlorries. Her hull was a similar design to the *Frozen Beauty* apart from the balloon system. Fanning did not understand the details, but with the two vehicles side by side it was clear that the *Blossom* had a smaller envelope overall, and that it stayed inflated while the ship sat in the grass.

There were two engineers checking the pipes and balloons as she approached. One of them noticed her and gave the usual double-take of someone who assumed she was male then decided they weren't so sure. This normally resulted in a stare, followed by the realisation that they were staring and a very deliberate (and obvious) looking away.

"Permission to come aboard!" Fanning shouted up. The older of the two engineers waved his hand at the cargo door at the rear.

Fanning shifted the box in her arms and walked around to the back of the vessel. She paused while a slick sheet of ice as thick as her arm and as big as a church window was winched carefully out. Bits of dirt and plant-life speckled the mostly clear block, clouded in places with other impurities.

The workers did not give her a second look. She was old news to them and they got paid by the job, so the sooner they finished the sooner they could move on to the next one.

She watched her footing on the icy floor as she made her way through the cold interior. The crewman releasing the next pile of ice for removal frowned at her.

"Captain?" she asked.

The crewman jerked his thumb at the stairs up to the bridge. The interior was the same design as the *Frozen Beauty*. Fanning climbed the steps, her hands freezing on the metal banister. She yanked open the first door and made her way through to the control room.

The captain of the *Blossom* was another Chinaman, probably about the same age as Captain Zang's first mate—what was his name? Dingbang? To the right was the navigator's station. The Babbage was covered with a sheet. Apparently they didn't have a computationer or didn't believe in them.

"Who you? What want?"

Fanning bowed low, holding the box in both hands. "Greetings, Captain Han, from Captain Qi Zang."

Han grunted and glanced at the chronometer on the wall.

"I am sorry for taking your time, Captain, but Captain Zang asks a boon."

There was no response from Han, but he kept his attention on her.

"She believes you will have the honour of receiving a visit from Kuan-Yin Sun." At that name Han's eyes narrowed. He did not look pleased. Fanning pressed on. "She asks that you hold this gift for Sun, along with the gift you have for him. To give to him when he arrives."

Han made no answer but continued to stare at Fanning. Qi had supposed they might reach an impasse, and had given Fanning a suggestion that might break it She tried it out. "Captain Qi knows how much you appreciated your time with Li Qin Yi, and suggests you might want to repeat that pleasure."

Captain Han stood up straighter and his gaze went from relaxed dislike to an intense study. It was not comfortable. The silence stretched out until Han grunted again and nodded towards the chart table.

Fanning carefully placed the box on the table and bowed again. She retreated to the door and made her escape. She preferred people who were talkative.

That was another stage of the captain's plan successfully carried out. Now for the next.

*   *   *

The sun was low enough in the sky to provide plenty of shadows as Qi, Kuan-Yin Sun, and his heavies made their way through the streets of Delhi towards the air-dock.

Sun poked his gun into her side, hitting a nerve and making her jerk sideways. "It is not on your ship, Zang. Do not think you can deceive me."

"Of course not, Kuan," she said, mirroring his use of her family name without honorific, by using his given name in a familiar way she did not feel. "I would not dream of trying to fool you in such a transparent way."

"You could not have hidden it."

"What's the hardest thing to find, Kuan-Yin Sun?"

"Don't waste my time with philosophical riddles."

Half a dozen children ran across the road in front of them, playing a game of tag. They paused for a moment, staring at the strange group. One of the younger ones stretched out his hand to beg. But an older girl had seen the way Sun held his hands and Qi's arm; she dragged the younger boy back and said something in the local language. The children ran on without a backward glance.

"I'm not wasting your time. The thing you cannot find is the thing that is not there." She turned her head towards him and smiled. "Your prize was never on the *Beauty*."

He frowned as he absorbed her words. She knew he wasn't stupid; this was the trickiest part of the plan.

"But you tried to sell it."

"Have you ever seen a magician at work? The way they make you look at one hand while doing the trick with the other?"

He thought it through. "You wanted me to think you'd sold it." She settled back but he wasn't finished. "Why?"

Yes. Why? That was a good question. She had hoped he wouldn't make it that far in the reasoning. "Who said I was selling your item?"

She held her breath. He said nothing. They came round a corner and saw the gate to the air-dock ahead of them.

"I can get you in, Sun, but not your friends."

"I still have the gun," he said as he placed it in a pocket, keeping his hand on it.

"That's not something I'd forget."

12

Qi could have made a run for it as they moved through the gaps between the administrative buildings. The comfortable life of an administrator—albeit for a crime gang—had made Sun soft. He might be able to put a bullet in her, but the risk of that at the air-dock, surrounded by the British? He was unlikely to try. However, running would not help; under no circumstances would she abandon the *Beauty*. She corrected herself: well, perhaps in death. But she had always imagined that she and the *Frozen Beauty* would die together.

She shook herself. No one was going to die today. If Fanning had completed her mission successfully and delivered the vase, all would be well.

The buildings of the air-dock had not been constructed with the usual flair of the British. They were brick rather than stone and had little ornamentation. Their most striking feature was the arches over the windows.

They stood to the side as a fleet of Army steamlorries huffed by. She was amused by the way Sun tried to hide his face. She had no qualms; she had always been honest with the British—even the Excise men. At least, she'd never been caught in a lie, and that was the same thing as honesty.

They came out onto the main field. The *Frozen Beauty*'s hot air envelopes were completely deflated and Remy had folded them neatly. It was always strange seeing the ship that way, as if she were naked. Set down close by was the *Cherry Blossom in Winter*; she was the same design as the *Beauty*, but Captain Han had kept her hydrogen balloons—an extra expense that Qi avoided by using Remy's hot-air design.

The *Blossom* was nearly unloaded. The cargo space was wide and almost warm. Only a few slabs remained. Dock workers exchanged furtive glances, but they knew who Sun was and they would not want to even admit to having seen him.

She glanced back at Sun. Now that they were inside the ship he had pulled the gun from his pocket and had it pointed at her spine.

"You really don't need that."

"I will be the judge of that, Zang."

She climbed the stairs towards the bridge. Strange, how the staircase differed from the one on her ship. Superficially they were the same, and yet this one moved differently, and creaked on different steps.

They pushed their way through the ice-lock doors and came into the main cabin. Han was at the chart table, already plotting his route back into the mountains. When he saw Qi enter, he hastily covered the map.

Ice was a precious commodity. Every captain had favourite sites from which to mine it and, come summer, those sites were even more carefully guarded. Of course, one could collect ice that had already been cut by ground crews. But then one had to have the money to pay them up-front, and there was always the risk they might hijack the ship instead.

Han came round the table; he spent a long moment looking at the gun in Sun's hand, then grunted at them. Qi was not sure she'd ever heard him utter more than five words at one time.

Han turned and bent down behind the chart table. Sun swung his gun round, trained on him. As Han straightened holding two boxes, he frowned at the gun barrel. He placed the boxes on the edge of the chart table, then backed to the window and crossed his arms over his chest, a scowl darkening his face.

Sun stared at the two boxes. While they were not large, there was no way he would be able to carry them and the gun simultaneously.

"Would you like me to carry those for you?" Qi asked pleasantly, moving forward to take them.

Sun jerked the gun up and pointed it at her stomach. "Back off!"

She did as she was instructed, her hands in front of her defensively. "I was only offering to help."

"I do not require your help. I do not trust you, Captain Qi."

For which I am truly grateful, she thought to herself.

Awkwardly Sun managed to scoop up the large boxes. His western suit had become creased, and the rough edges of the boxes dug into it. One wrong move and the material might tear. He rested them on his gun arm, so he could for the most part point the weapon in her direction.

"Don't follow me," he said to her and then glanced at Han. "Keep her here for an hour."

Han grunted.

"What about the *Beauty*?" Qi said quickly. "I need to be out of here for the next trip."

"I'll send a message, Zang."

"Write a letter now."

Sun turned and sneered at her. "Don't you trust me?"

"Write me a letter now, Sun. You wouldn't want Captain Han here to think you're untrustworthy and spread it around, would you? You know how he gossips."

Sun returned to the desk, acquired paper and pen from Captain Han, and wrote out his instructions in English. He picked up the boxes again, made his way to the door, and left. Not a word was exchanged.

As the door swung shut Qi put her hand into a pocket. Han jerked back defensively, then grinned as she pulled out a metal flask. "Scotch?"

Han grunted.

13

Kuan-Yin Sun emerged from the cargo hold of the *Blossom*, awkwardly carrying the two boxes. He co-opted one of the ground crew to carry them for him. From his place at the whist game, Fanning watched as Sun adjusted the weight of his gun in his pocket as he strode between the buildings towards the main exit.

Fanning put down his cards on the tea chest they were using as a table and made quick good-byes to the other players. They were not pleased at his sudden departure; there was money they wanted to win back. Fanning tore himself away with hasty promises of his return as Sun disappeared from view.

As Fanning rounded the building he saw that Sun was getting away from him. The lad put on a spurt of speed. He was fairly sure that Sun wouldn't recognise him, but it would not look good if Sun noticed him in pursuit. As long as Sun didn't turn around, there wouldn't be a problem.

Looking ahead towards the main entrance, he was pleased to see an open carriage waiting just beyond the wrought-iron gates. A woman held the reins. Good, she had arrived.

There had been no certainty she would be brave enough to come at all. This was not a task for the faint-hearted, but the rewards would be worth it, and now she had a personal stake in getting *Frozen Beauty* into the air.

Once outside the gates Sun hailed a hansom cab, gave the dock-worker something for his trouble, and climbed in with his boxes. Mrs Cameron looked delightful in the afternoon sunlight, in her cream and blue dress and matching bonnet with a veil pulled down over her left eye. That she should be married to such a man was a terrible crime and one they could now put right.

The hansom cab drew away; Sun must have given the driver instructions to move quickly, but Fanning was not too concerned. He had a pretty good idea which direction the criminal would be heading.

On seeing him approaching the gates, Mrs Cameron urged her horse into motion. As the carriage passed, Fanning swung up into the seat beside her. If she were not a married woman he would be happy with a kiss from those sweet lips.

She caught him staring, but he didn't look away as would have been polite. He wasn't British, so he just grinned—and she blushed.

"Follow that hansom, Mrs Cameron."

She focused her attention on the road, gave the reins a flick, and the pony stepped up its gait to a fast trot. Her driving skills equalled those of the cabbie. Fanning looked behind and saw another carriage following them. Men overflowed its seats, hanging from the sides and back. If he was not mistaken, one of those clinging to the side was the estimable Constable Templeton.

They followed the cab through the streets of Delhi. The cab kept to the main streets and avoided the more dangerous areas. The streets were not busy, but there was sufficient traffic to disguise their pursuit.

* * *

Kuan-Yin Sun sat back in the hansom cab. He should be pleased with himself; he had succeeded in making Qi Zang toe the line. If just one of these pilots got away with public disobedience, there would be no end of trouble.

He should be pleased, but he was not. Something was wrong. It was a feeling deep inside, a disturbance in his chi. Qi Zang had always had this effect on him, even before her father had died.

She rebelled against everything. Even the social station of a woman. Her father had been of a good family, and yet he had not bound her feet. She walked like a man. She dressed like a man.

And yet, Sun still lusted after her. He liked to think that he was above such things but he was not fool enough to be dishonest with himself. Despite her social disobedience—perhaps because of it—he was attracted to her.

He pushed the thought aside. This was not important. What was important now lay beneath his hand. He had regained the property he required in spite of her—and still he felt uncomfortable.

The hansom cab left the commercial district, crossed the river, and climbed into the better quality residences. The Family provided a decent property for him; it was not his own, but as long as he maintained control it would remain in his possession.

He entered the main living room and had his man place the boxes on a table that had been covered with a rough cloth to protect its polished surface. Pulling Han's box in front of him, he prised open the lid and pulled out a beautiful small statue of Confucius, the architect of Modern China. It was a good piece and would sell quite well.

Then came Qi's box, the battle he had had to get it made it seem more valuable. He lifted the lid and ran his hands through the protective straw; his fingers touched something small with a cool, smooth surface. Carefully he brought it out into the light: A delicate vase, Meiping if he was not mistaken, with strong blues showing the signs of the zodiac. No wonder Qi had wanted to hang on to it; this would fetch a very pretty price, enough for several trips.

Or it would have, if Qi had sold it herself.

A sudden banging on the door interrupted his thoughts. Sun frowned. He wanted to set the vase on the desk and enjoy its aesthetic *Beauty* for a time. This was one piece that would be going into his private collection.

The banging repeated and then ceased. His manservant came through almost at a run, with a westerner in a cheap suit directly behind him and, following him, two uniformed police officers.

The manservant threw himself to the floor in prostration.

"Kuan-Yin Sun? I am arresting you for the theft of certain valuable properties."

Sun felt a wave of fear run through him. Theft? Yes, of course, there was theft but not from anyone in Delhi. What trick was this?

The fellow in the suit strode over and looked down at the vase on the table. He gestured behind him and an Englishwoman came forward, accompanied by a boy—no, a girl. Another abominable female dressed in men's clothing.

"Mrs Cameron, do you see anything you recognise in this room?"

The woman stood with head downturned, hands clutched to keep them from shaking. Sun relaxed; he fixed her with his gaze, sneered, and drew his hands into fists. At that she lifted her head, and her gaze became harder, more certain. She looked directly at the vase on the table between them. Sun frowned. She wouldn't dare.

She raised her arm and pointed at the vase. "That belongs to my husband."

14

Captain Qi Zang stood on the bridge of the *Frozen Beauty*. The deck throbbed with the power of the furnace. She could feel the ship coming alive as the super-heated steam flowed through the pipes and into the seven balloons, heating the air and expanding it until the envelopes bulged with lift.

The generators hummed. The Faraday grid was ready to receive the electrical power that would cancel out gravity and allow them to lift.

The ship was ready to depart, but they were forced to wait. Out on the field a horse-drawn hansom rolled towards them at a rapid pace, carrying the passenger and the new crew member.

* * *

The cabbie brought the rig round the *Frozen Beauty* at an angle, so the blinkered horse would not be scared by the shifting and twisting balloons above the ship.

Smoke pumped steadily from the stack and steam escaped from some of the pipe joints. The ship appeared to be making ready to lift. It was not that Fanning disbelieved Captain Qi—she knew the captain would wait, as she had given her word—but Fanning had been betrayed more than once in both her lives, and the experiments of Dr Munroe had not been the first of those betrayals. Trusting did not come easily any longer.

The hansom came to a stop and Fanning swung down, holding out a hand to assist Mrs Cameron so that she did not trip on the hem of her long and impractical dress.

The woman looked at the *Beauty* with some concern. It was true the ship was not a passenger vessel and would not provide all the comforts of home. But it was an escape from her boorish and dangerous husband. The captain had offered Mrs Cameron—Beatrice—free passage to any port in exchange for her assistance in saving the *Beauty* from the hands of Kuan-Yin Sun.

Fanning went to the back of the hansom where the driver had unloaded the baggage. One small case for Fanning, and two cases and a trunk for Beatrice. Fanning piled the cases on the trunk and, with the driver, lifted them all together and headed for the ship.

Beatrice lifted one of the smaller cases from the trunk. It did not make a great deal of difference to the bearers, but they smiled politely regardless.

* * *

Mrs Beatrice Cameron stared at the gaudily coloured ship; the entire hull had been painted in bright blue with flowing white figures, accented by flowers and Chinese characters in brilliant red. Fanning had told her the vessel was christened the *Frozen Beauty*; the colours reminded her of winter snow and ice and blood. It had been years since Jeremy had brought her out to India, and that long since she had seen a real winter. Delhi was hot all the time, and worse when it rained.

She glanced up as she saw a movement against the blue sky. A man stood on the top deck, looking down. She looked away in embarrassment. He was stripped to the waist, revealing lithe musculature. He did not look at all rough, and both the hair on his head and his moustache were neatly trimmed in a cut she thought might be French.

They moved into the shadow of the ship and out of the sun. From a wide door—presumably used when loading and unloading the ice—a thin man in British army khaki scurried. His bold moustache would have suited any military man. Thankfully he was wearing a shirt, albeit with rolled-up sleeves, undone at the neck and discoloured with his perspiration.

So many men, almost pirates, and she was willingly going on board. Still, Fanning said the captain was a woman. That idea still resounded in Beatrice's mind: The captain is a woman. And a Chinese. A woman in charge of a sky vessel. It was like a story. As if she had opened a book by H G Wells, Conan Doyle or Jules Verne, and stepped into its pages.

Fanning and the driver put down the trunk. The wiry man took the driver's place; his muscles bulged as he lifted the weight at his end. Fanning once again took the strain at the other.

Beatrice caught herself staring again. What would Jeremy say?

Her thoughts lingered briefly on her ne'er-do-well husband. It did not matter what Jeremy thought anymore. He was just a memory. Let him see how he would manage without her support. She was taking ship with ice pirates.

*　*　*

Captain Qi was informed that the passengers' gear had been stowed. Accommodations had been tricky to organise, as they only had one spare cabin and it was quite small. In the end she had decided to put Fanning in that one, and have Mrs Cameron share with her.

It was better than the other way around. Though it was clear Fanning had the body of a woman, she insisted on behaving like a man, which made bunking with her … him … feel somewhat awkward.

Both of them stood on the bridge behind her.

Otto had programmed the Babbage and a course had been decided. Steam pressure was high; *Monsieur* Darras reported the balloon envelopes to be tight.

"Faraday in one minute," she said. Dingbang operated the steam klaxon that sounded both inside and outside the ship. The ground crew released the remaining hawsers at the prow and stern. Tying the ship down was an antiquated concept, since the vessel would go nowhere until the Faraday was engaged. Still, the British felt better following their rules—no matter how out of date.

The letter written by Kuan-Yin Sun had ordered the *Frozen Beauty* restocked and refuelled. With the money they had made from selling the vase, even after having paid Mrs Cameron her share, they could afford to seek new trading grounds without taking a cargo this time around.

But it just felt wrong for a trading vessel to travel without a cargo, so she had managed to get some trade goods to carry south. Their first stop would be Kerala, on the southeast coast.

"Captain?"

Ding broke her out of her reverie; the minute was long past. At her signal he gave another quick burst on the klaxon. She counted to ten and engaged the Faraday device.

She felt the comforting lightening and the ship floated up from the ground, gathering speed. Qi engaged the driving rotors. The *Beauty*, light of any significant cargo, shot away like a tiger through the grass.

As Qi spun the helm the ship turned like a sailing vessel in a strong breeze, leaping away to the south. And Qi's heart leapt with her.

BOOK 2

LADIES' DAY

1

Captain Qi Zang clawed her way from the trapdoor onto the upper deck of the *Frozen Beauty*. Rain lashed her and she was soaked before she was even halfway out. The wind ripped the trapdoor from her fingers and slammed it flat against the deck.

Being on the ship in a rain storm was uncanny. The Faraday device had the strangest effect on rain, causing it to fall at a fraction of its usual speed. But it had no effect on the wind. So the gale still drove the rain which, with almost no inclination to fall, came from the side. Where it landed, it collected in huge, slow-moving globules.

The whole ship swung to port as a gust caught it. She was glad she couldn't see far. It was early evening and, by rights, the sun should have been lighting up the pass that would guide them into Kerala. Monsoon hadn't started yet but this storm wasn't waiting.

The winds built up across the Indian Ocean and picked up their water. They hit the mountains on this side of the Indian sub-continent and dropped that moisture. On most days it was just rain. This time the gods had decided to battle it out around them.

She pulled herself up and allowed her weight to carry her to the central superstructure across the tilting deck before the wind decided to slam the trapdoor back on her. With one hand gripping the edge of the balloon shed, she reached down and pulled the trapdoor up and over. The wind caught it again but she hung on, then slid the latch into place.

The deck swung back and she clung on to stop herself from falling toward the rail. She had given orders to Dingbang to keep them running along the centre of the valley. She wanted more height. They were below the level of the mountains and risked running straight into a cliff, but Remy wasn't answering the whistle of the communications tube.

Otto had offered to go instead of her, as had Fanning, but Otto was too young to know what to do if Remy was in trouble, and Fanning was just a girl. Even if she thought she was a boy.

Besides it was her ship and if anyone was going to deal with the possibility that Remy was hurt, dead or simply lost overboard—which meant dead—it would be her.

She staggered along the wall of the balloon shed. The *Beauty* swung again, caught her off balance and slammed her into the wall. She swung round the corner into the relative calm between the shed and the smoke-stack housing. She cursed in Mandarin.

"That is not very ladylike, Madame *Capitaine*," drawled Remy Darras. He was wearing wet weather gear: a big oiled cape and a sou'wester. For once he did not look every inch a French gentleman as he usually did.

"We need more altitude," she shouted. The whole ship lit up in black and white relief from a flash of lightning. The thunder rolled over them like gigantic wave.

She thanked whatever gods were listening that she had taken on Remy Darras and accepted his advice to switch from hydrogen to hot air. In a thunderstorm the lightning could make a hydrogen balloon explode. The *Beauty* would be the only ship in the sky at a time like this—which was a small mercy—except for perhaps one of the British ships that didn't use balloons at all.

She pointed upwards. "More height, Monsieur Darras!"

"*Oui*, madame!"

He pulled open the door to his shack and allowed the swing of the ship to carry him inside. Qi followed him in and shut the door. The noise of the wind screaming through the rigging did not diminish, but the driven rain was held at bay.

The ship surged upwards and they both staggered. She hoped it was just a random updraft and did not indicate they were closer to a cliff. She glanced at the seven sets of dials that showed the pressure of the *Beauty*'s seven balloon envelopes. The needles oscillated wildly as the balloons were buffeted by the wind. She could even follow a gust as it hit the balloons one after the other, twitching the needles as it travelled the length of the ship.

White light burst round the edges of the door and through the windows and cracks in the ceiling, the needle on the dial monitoring the second balloon from the end suddenly flopped over to zero, the ship lurched and Qi felt lighter than usual.

"*Mon dieu*," cried Remy and leapt to the valves on the steam pipes. He spun the one under the zeroed dial. The two of them froze as they listened to the super-heated steam screaming through the pipe. The dial did not even flutter.

"Close that, open others," shouted Qi, and she leapt for the valve nearest her. Remy spun the other back and closed it off as she got the first open and started on its neighbour.

"Not too much pressure, *Capitaine*, they will rupture. I will do it!"

Qi paused. Remy knew his equipment better than she. She headed out and clambered back towards the trapdoor. A wall of rock loomed up on the left, less than fifty yards away. An abrupt gust tossed them towards it. She saw the port thruster spinning to push them away from the cliff. Its efforts were almost useless against the raging storm until an updraft lifted the prow and turned the ship away.

It could easily have gone the other way.

She managed to get the trapdoor up, squeezed down until her feet reached touched the ladder, then slipped and fell the rest of the way. Under reduced gravity she sustained only a bruised elbow and slightly damaged pride.

She had not had a chance to latch the trapdoor; the wind flung it open, letting in the storm and a unhurried flurry of icy water. She headed forward and slammed open the door to the bridge.

Ding wrestled with the helm, with Fanning helping him hold the wheel. Mrs Cameron and Otto were nowhere to be seen. Qi strode forward.

"I'll take the helm," she ordered as another lightning flash streaked down near them and thunder exploded. Fanning continued to cling to the helm as if her life depended on it. Perhaps it did. Ding stepped to one side to allow Qi space to take the wheel, but he too continued to hold it even when she placed both hands on it.

"What happened?" said Ding.

Qi glanced round. Mrs Cameron was on the floor tending to Otto, who looked to be unconscious.

"One of the envelopes ruptured. We're going down."

2

Qi, with Fanning in tow, walked away from where the *Beauty* lay. They clambered over rocks that had tumbled from the mountainside above them at some distant time in the past, now overgrown with moss and ferns. The sky was filled with broken clouds being driven north by a wind that could not be felt at ground level.

The sun was high. The storm had raged the rest of the night, long after they had come down hard. The moment they had touched down Qi disengaged the Faraday device to ensure they stayed put. Remy had vented all the hot air and, with the help of the crew, pulled in the deflated balloons as best he could. They had lashed them down but there was always the risk of the wind getting into them.

The crew had suffered through the rest of the night. Otto had regained consciousness and Mrs Cameron had moved him to his cabin where she stayed with him until daybreak. Whether the others had slept Qi did not know for sure. She had not. The fear the winds might rip the balloons to shreds preyed on her mind. If they could not be reinflated the *Beauty* would be stranded.

Remy and Terry Montgomery were in the process of checking the integrity of each of the balloon envelopes with Ichiro assisting.

Qi continued higher. It had been many years since she had climbed on rocks. Back at school in China, the nuns had had very strong ideas about what was proper behaviour for boys and girls. If a boy had a scraped knee it might be overlooked, and he might get away with a scolding. But if a girl should have a scraped knee? That was a caning offence. Young ladies did not do things that might result in their knees being scraped.

But Qi had done so. The Roman Catholic school had been built just outside the town, and there were hills to be climbed on both sides beyond the rice terraces. Her father was gone for months at a time, and she had to fend for herself. Sometimes—often—that meant fighting.

Her foot slipped on some moss, and she was brought back to the world with a jolt. She glanced around and decided she was high enough. Fanning was a few yards below, still climbing.

Qi turned to survey the scene and get some idea of where they were. Back the way they had come the valley twisted back and forth, gaining height fast. The terrain was uneven and strewn with huge rocks. If they had hit the deck any sooner, *Beauty*'s back would have been broken.

As it was, the ship rested on a flat swampy space where the river had burst its banks and occupied the small shelf area. It was far too close to the edge that dropped a further hundred or more feet to the valley below. All around them were the mountains that bordered the northern and eastern regions of Kerala. They did not even come close to rivalling the Himalayas, but they were tall enough to present a major barrier to travel—and to shelter less savoury individuals.

She could see Remy and the others at work on the top deck. And, as she watched, Beatrice Cameron—in full dress with a parasol—stepped delicately down the cargo ramp and picked her way across the stones, avoiding the water.

She looked completely out of place.

Qi pulled out her telescope and surveyed the lower valley. A track threaded its way between rice fields. There were shacks here and there, but these would not be for families. They were only temporary shelters for those working out in the paddies, where even now people were moving around. Around the borders of the paddies were fields with different crops, which she could not name at this distance.

Her attention was attracted by a line of rising smoke that had not been there a moment before. Along the track from the southeast came a puffing steam engine of some sort. She trained her telescope on it. She was not familiar with the design, but the artillery piece mounted above heavy duty tracks identified its purpose.

Moving along behind was a squad of infantry, in the khaki uniforms the British Army had adopted in recent years.

There was only one reason for it to be out here, and *Beauty* was that reason. The locals would immediately send for assistance if something they did not understand came their way.

Fanning had just reached her and was staring in the same direction.

"Let's go," said Qi. "We need to stop them before they get itchy trigger fingers." She would have been happy to dodge their gun if *Beauty* had been airworthy, but right now she was a sitting duck. She guessed they had about thirty minutes, as long as these men were sufficiently intelligent to ask questions first.

With Fanning behind her, Qi jumped from stone to stone in her hurry to get down. Once she reached level ground she set off at a jog back to the ship. Mrs Cameron was standing at the edge of the drop-off looking out towards their welcoming committee.

As she approached she saw Ding and Terry mounting the flag mast on the front of the *Beauty*. There was generally no need to have the mast erected, but it was kept for tradition.

She left Fanning to fetch Mrs Cameron and climbed a ladder mounted on the outside of the ship, then rushed across the deck as the mast was being lashed in position. The flag locker had been dragged up on deck. She threw it open and sorted quickly through the contents. The inside lid of the locker displayed a key showing their meanings, but those maritime meanings had not been updated for flying vessels.

She pulled out the red diamond on the white background and threw it to Ding. He pulled it open and stared at it.

"*I am disabled; communicate with me,*" said Qi. Ding nodded, attached it to the line, and then rapidly pulled it into the air. There was sufficient wind to make it flap limply.

At that moment something whistled overhead and exploded into the rocks behind them. A thunderous roar filled the air, and bits of stone rained down on them.

Qi dived for cover, hoping none of the envelopes would be damaged.

3

She had the idea that the steering thruster was running out of control because her ears were filled with a high-pitched whine. She lifted her head from the rocks. A pall of smoke and rock dust drifted across the tumbled stones on the slope. She coughed into the dry air.

The cough sounded strangely distant and she realised the whining was only in her ears. She brushed her hair back from her face and looked towards the approaching artillery car. It had not fired again. Perhaps the soldiers did not understand nautical flags. Why should they.

There was a movement down the slope from her; she saw Fanning pushing herself up from the rocks. Qi stumbled down the hill.

"Are you all right?"

Fanning looked up and grinned. "Sure packed a punch." She was almost shouting. "You okay, Cap?"

Fanning reached out and touched her cheek. Qi was confused; it was such an intimate action, in the wrong time and place. But when Fanning withdrew her hand it glistened with red. "Best come down and let the lady take a look at it." She wiped her hand on a dusty white kerchief she pulled from a pocket and held out her hand.

It was crazy the way the young girl took charge like a man, but it made climbing down off the stones easier.

Before they hit the level Qi stopped again and looked out across the valley. The column of men, cavalry and artillery was still moving in their direction but the muzzle of the big gun was no longer pointed in their direction.

* * *

"What's the situation, Remy?"

"It is not good, *Capitaine*," the Frenchman said. Qi had never seen him looking so dirty and tired; he usually took so much pride in his appearance. Behind him the bulk of Ichiro contrasted with the thin frame of Terry Montgomery but both of them looked concerned.

Qi hissed and pulled back, as Mrs Cameron applied some stinging unguent to the cut that marked her face from her right ear and across her cheek.

"You'll have a scar if you don't let me do this, Captain."

She sounded like Sister Mary Therese, who had been in charge of the school infirmary. A lifetime of instant obedience made Qi settle and allow the woman, who was no older than she, have her way. Whatever the stuff was, it stung badly. Still, Mrs Cameron was more delicate than Dingbang.

Qi turned her attention back to Remy. "What do you need to get us back in the air?"

"You come with me." Remy offered his hand to help her up

"Stay right where you are, I haven't finished," said Mrs Cameron. Remy dropped his hand. "Another minute, Captain."

The woman began to clean her face with a damp cloth. Qi frowned and then winced as the cloth pulled at something embedded in her skin. Mrs Cameron pulled out a pair of tweezers and pried loose a sliver of metal that had penetrated a layer of skin. The place immediately stung and Qi internally cursed the perversity of bodies. Qi sat obedient and still as Mrs Cameron cleaned the rest of her face. No more shards were found.

Ding had been standing on the drop-off into the valley, watching the approaching column. He turned from the edge and made his way across the stones to the group.

"Five minutes, riders come," he said.

A sigh escaped Qi's lips and she looked at the expectant faces of her crew. "Fanning, you go with Remy. Make a list of everything we need to get *Beauty* aloft. Ding, take Ichiro and greet them as far down the track as you can."

"We will be weaponless, *mèimei*," said Ding, looking down at her. He only called her 'little sister' when he was worried.

"What choice do we have, old man? Bring them up slowly if you can, and I will meet the welcoming committee." Ding gave a short bow and headed off, pausing only to gather up Ichiro, who loomed behind him, as they headed off round the other side of the ship.

She turned to Mrs Cameron. "How do I look?"

The woman sniffed. "Damaged. Untidy. Dirty. Your hair needs doing, and"—she paused as if deciding how to say something—"you've been wearing the same clothes since we left Delhi. Two days."

"You mean I smell?"

"It wouldn't be polite to say."

"Calling me dirty is polite?"

The woman shrugged and smiled. She climbed to her feet and offered her hand to help Qi up. Qi accepted the assistance. Her muscles were stiff from sitting. It wasn't just that she'd been in the same clothes for two days. She'd barely slept, and meals had been irregular.

Mrs Cameron managed to appear perfect, but then she did not have to run the ship in a storm.

Fanning and Remy had reached the *Beauty* and were climbing one of the ladders mounted on the outside of the hull. Ding and Ichiro were out of sight.

"We'll say you chartered the ship to bring you south," said Qi. "You do the talking."

Qi found the look of fear and astonishment in Mrs Cameron's face amusing. Revenge could be sweet.

"I can't do that," she said. "I mean, why would I do that?" Mrs Cameron looked across at the *Beauty* resting on the edge of the river's flood plain. It might be gaily painted but it was not a pretty vessel. Just an ice cargo ship: squat and functional. "I mean, why wouldn't I just take a scheduled air-ship?"

"Don't you know how to lie?"

Mrs Beatrice Cameron opened her mouth to respond but no words came out.

The woman's previous comments made Qi uncomfortable and conscious of her unkempt state. She found the cloth Mrs Cameron had used to wipe her face, soaked it in one of the streams of overflowing river water and wiped the rest of her face and hands, then started on the leather of her jacket and trousers.

She decided to put Beatrice out of her misery. "Stick to the truth."

"That I left my husband? I can't tell them that."

"No, but if you have that as the reason you needed to get out of Delhi so quickly, and say that you hired me—which, in a way, you did—then you won't get caught in a lie. You'll be a woman of mystery."

At that moment Ding reappeared, Ichiro at his shoulder and followed by five men leading their mounts. They splashed through the river's streams and pools in their direction.

Beatrice glanced at Qi, lifted her chin and walked steadily towards them, Qi following close behind.

4

Captain Hillary Reynolds followed the Chinaman and the huge Nipponese up the slope towards the stranded ship. It had been lucky for them that one of the older men under his command had previously worked in the merchant navy and recognised the flags the ship had run up.

It certainly had been a hellish storm in the mountains last night; little wonder they had been downed. And lucky they hadn't been smashed to bits against the mountainside.

The Chinaman (he'd introduced himself as *Ding* something or other), the First Mate apparently, was difficult to understand as his English was quite poor. The Japanese fellow said nothing at all. Just loomed.

After Reynolds chose a squad of four men, they all proceeded up the slope. The river water was cascading dramatically down the valley, swamping the rice fields. The peasants were out trying to reduce the potential damage. Rice was a queer crop but he had no complaints about what could be done with it.

The peasants had alerted them to the presence of the vessel. Being peasants, they had grossly overstated both the size and the weaponry of the ship. He did not recognise the type of vessel as they approached and he really had not been able to understand the name the Chinaman had used for it. He couldn't see any weapons at all.

Still, it did not matter. Mrs Ruane had commanded the crew should be detained to ensure they were not connected with the rebels. They reached the flat river bed and made their way around the ship, stepping across the stones.

To his consternation, he found himself face-to-face with two women: a woman as white and appropriately dressed as Mrs Ruane, and another Chinese, a woman in men's clothing. However, he gathered his composure and called out in his parade-ground voice.

*　*　*

Qi studied the British officer. He was a Caucasian in his late twenties, wearing the khaki uniform of the British Indian Army. He was not holding his pistol, but its holster was unbuttoned. He clutched a swagger stick in his right hand. The threat was clear enough. Three of the four Sikh soldiers in his squad held their rifles ready, while the fourth hung back with the horses. They were not watching the exchange between their officer and the women; they were watching the rocks behind, as well as the crew.

"You will surrender your vessel to me and consider yourself detained under my authority."

"I beg your pardon, Captain …?" Mrs Cameron's voice carried a tone of authority Qi had not been expecting. The soldier hesitated for a moment.

"Captain Reynolds, madam." He cleared his throat. "Suspected bandits are to be detained pending investigations."

"I look like a bandit, do I, Captain Reynolds?"

"Of course not, madam. However, these"—he indicated the ship's crew with a wave of his stick—"look very much like bandits."

Beatrice Cameron smiled. "And you think I would be in the company of bandits, Captain Reynolds?"

"You might be a prisoner."

"This is Captain Qi Zang" (she emphasised the title to ensure there was no mistake) "of the *Frozen Beauty*, an ice cargo vessel. These others are her crew."

"And you are, madam?"

"Mrs Beatrice Cameron, late of Delhi. I must get to the Fortress in Ceylon, and I required a ship. This was the only method of transport available where I considered I would be safe—if you take my meaning."

The army captain stared at Qi Zang, who acknowledged him with a nod of her head. He understood Mrs Cameron's unspoken point: A female travelling alone would feel safer aboard a ship captained by a woman.

"You will vouch for them?"

"Captain, we would not even be here if the ship had not been injured in the storm last night. Captain Qi is in need of materials for repair." She was getting into her stride. "Quite frankly, Captain, I am quite put out by this delay, and to be treated as a common criminal rather takes the biscuit. Now if you and your men would care to *assist* me instead of presenting a problem, I would be most grateful."

Captain Reynolds, however, was not so easily deflected. "Naturally, Mrs Cameron, you are not under arrest. However my orders are clear. You, Captain Qi and the crew must accompany me to the barracks."

Qi spoke up. "I'm afraid I can't agree, Captain. My vessel must be repaired as soon as possible. We have a schedule and we are already late."

If Captain Reynolds was surprised by her command of English, he did not show it. "I do not wish to be indelicate, madam, but I must insist. Once your *bona fides* have been established you may repair your ship and depart."

As their argument had intensified Remy, Otto, Terry and Fanning had come to the railing on the top deck and were looking down. Qi glanced at them. Terry in particular was looking at her hard. Qi was aware he would not be willing to go. He and the British

Army had a history. He had not told her what it was and she would never pry, though since she had found him in China it probably had something to do the Boxer Rebellion.

"Captains," Mrs Cameron interrupted. "I'm sure we can come to some arrangement."

"I will not leave my ship unmanned." Qi glared at him. "Four of my people will remain to guard the ship and make repairs. Shoot me if you must."

"You could leave a guard," said Mrs Cameron before Captain Reynolds had a chance to argue further.

The officer hesitated for a moment. "Very well. You can leave three but I will require their names."

5

The British captain had permitted Mrs Cameron to ride in the artillery carriage that had accompanied the troop. Qi and the rest of the crew had to walk with mounted soldiers behind them.

They followed the track that led between the rice fields and the other crops further up the hillside. The peasants in the fields paused in their work and leaned on their tools to watch the procession pass by.

Qi glanced back one final time at the *Beauty* perched precariously on the edge of the high river bed—she could see Terry, Remy and Ichiro watching them—before it disappeared from sight as they rounded a bend in the valley. Behind her tramped Dingbang, Otto and Fanning, who had drawn the usual double-takes from those who had never seen the like of her before.

The fields continued and then ran up against a thick wood. From behind the trees a thin line of smoke rose into the now still air.

Captain Reynolds walked his horse alongside them.

"How are you planning on verifying our *bona fides*, Captain?" she asked.

"Copies of all relevant records are held at the main air-docks in the city. We will take your details and send a man to check them."

"And how long will that take?"

"We should receive a reply by tomorrow at the earliest, perhaps the next day."

Qi had decided not to antagonise their captor since it would probably be unhelpful in the circumstances. Although the British were sticklers for detail, they were efficient enough. The delay

irritated her but the repairs had to be done. She had the list of
requirements from Remy and Terry.

"And where will we be staying?"

"Mrs Cameron will be invited to stay at the house I expect. We
have suitable accommodation for suspected bandits."

"You're going to put us in *cells*?"

He at least had the manners to look slightly embarrassed. "They
are not prison."

She said nothing for a while but trudged along the track. She had
long since given up trying to avoid the mud and squelched through
an area where the thinly distributed cobblestones had subsided into
the field.

"Who owns the house?"

"The Ruane family."

The name meant nothing to Qi, but then she did not have a
need to keep up on well-to-do British families, and said as much.

"The family is Irish."

*   *   *

It was coming on to midday when they broke through the wood and
crossed a flat grassy area with not the slightest bush or shrub. Here
and there across its surface she could see light reflecting on pools.
Ahead of them was a crenelated wall that looked as if it could
withstand the attack of an army.

It was apparent the threat of attack from bandits was taken
seriously and the open space they now crossed was a killing field for
any force attacking from the mountains.

But if the bandits had an airship of any sort then the woods,
open space and wall were nothing more than an empty threat.

The track approached within twenty feet of the wall and then turned parallel to it. As the only safe path through the mire, its attractiveness was another trap.

Finally it closed on the wall and intersected it at a solid gate of oak and iron. It was open but they had been under observation for some time from the lookout above it. Had they been attackers, the closed gate would have presented almost as much defence as the stone wall itself.

* * *

Beatrice was grateful when the artillery carriage came to a complete stop outside the gates. The constant noise from its huffing steam engine and the grinding of the metal wheels on the stones of the path had made any sort of conversation, even with the driver next to her, quite impossible—even if she could have thought of something to say to the fellow.

The driver disengaged something and the noise level dropped considerably. Then he rotated a lever a few times until it seemed to resist him and came to a stop. Perhaps it prevented the wheels from moving, though she could not imagine any force on God's Earth that could force it to move except its own colossal, and extremely noisy, engine.

Satisfied, the driver clambered to the door and opened it. She climbed carefully to her feet; she was small enough to stand upright in the cabin but the constant vibration of the machine seemed to have had a bad effect on her strength and balance.

She held on to the open door as she climbed down the steps. Fanning was there and stretched out her hand. "Grab hold, Beatrice." She was grateful for the support and finally made it down. She staggered for a moment but Fanning tucked her arm behind her elbow.

"I got ya."

"I think I may walk next time."

"Better get you something a little more practical then," said Fanning with a grin. "Those skirts and fancy shoes wouldn't last half the distance."

Beatrice shook her head. She still could not manage the strange duality of Fanning, the male attitude in the female body. Sometimes it was better just to think of her as him.

They made their way across to the rest of the group, with Fanning taking the lead, of course.

Captain Reynolds stepped forwards. "If you'd like to walk ahead with me, Mrs Cameron?"

Beatrice glanced at the others, surrounded by casual but alert soldiers. Not close enough to be oppressive but the intent was clear .

"Thank you, Captain, but I will walk with the crew."

"As you wish."

And with their armed escort they headed up towards the house. Behind them the artillery carriage fired up again and, with a roar of steam, headed away.

6

The track wound through an apple orchard that hid the buildings ahead for a short while. They passed through another gate, this one in a low stone wall that separated the orchard from carefully tended gardens.

Away to their right, the north, were a series of utilitarian buildings. Rising up in front of them was the smoke and steam from the still audible puffing of the artillery carriage. *Probably the barracks for the soldiers*, thought Qi.

Ahead and slightly to the south was the mansion, built in a combination of British and Indian Gothic. Tall glazed windows with wide vertical separation gave light to the lower three airy floors, and further windows in the roof areas illuminated rooms for the staff.

The family must be very rich to maintain such a place.

The light of the day was too bright to allow her to see into the rooms but she had been in places like this before. It would be marble and oak, high ceilings and steam-driven *punkhas* to keep the air circulating. There would be Indian staff in every room to wait, hand and foot, on the ageing bastions of the British ruling elite.

She was glad she was not part of this world. Unlike Beatrice. Qi glanced across at the woman. She had chosen to walk with them, which had seemed odd in a way—but then, they had rescued her and perhaps she felt she owed them a debt. Though, if anything, the debt was in the other direction. If not for Beatrice, she would have lost the *Beauty*.

The party circled around the building. The path changed from a muddy track to clean gravel that crunched beneath their boots and shoes. The Indian gardeners—so many of them and of so many different ages—watched the strange parade as it passed them by. Qi laughed to herself at the sight they must make.

"Something funny, Cap?" asked Fanning. Qi flushed and shook her head.

"Just a thought."

She glanced to the other side where Dingbang was watching her with his look of serious concern. Qi shook herself. He was right; this was potentially dangerous. They needed to get out of here as quickly as they could.

The garden at the front of the house was a glorious riot of flowers, plants with leaves of purple, blue and grey interspersed with pools and streams over which hung willows. Paths traced and criss-crossed through the whole chaotic mix.

Mrs Cameron stopped and stared. "It's so beautiful."

"Thank you."

The voice came from behind them. The whole party turned and gawped. *This must be the lady of the house,* thought Qi. Mrs Kathleen Ruane was certainly a very striking woman. She was taller than most men. Her red hair was in a thick braid that hung across her shoulder. A white, wide-brimmed hat shaded both her face and her bare freckled shoulders from the sun. Her dress was practical rather than decorative. She wore leather gloves and carried a wicker basket that held small digging tools.

When she stepped among them Qi had the impression of looking up at a giantess. The soldiers put up their guns and glanced at the captain.

"Are these our bandits, Captain Reynolds?" There was a laugh in her voice along with a tone of absolute command.

He saluted. "Yes, Mrs Ruane." He hesitated. "If you would not mind stepping away from the prisoners so my men can keep their guns trained."

Mrs Ruane ignored him. She looked at each of them, pausing only on Fanning. She finally turned to Qi. "You are their leader?"

Her words carried a soft lilt of an accent Qi did not recognise. "Captain Qi Zang … Mrs Ruane."

The woman smiled at her. "Excellent. And these are all your crew?"

"All save our passenger, Mrs Cameron."

Beatrice Cameron seemed as taken with the impressive Mrs Ruane as Fanning, both of them quite captivated. Qi glanced at Dingbang and Otto; the latter looked as if his tongue might roll out of his mouth if it were not shut. Even Dingbang's attention was fixed.

Qi frowned.

"Mrs Ruane, we are not bandits, we are traders, and we would like to be away as soon as possible. If that is possible."

The woman took as much notice of her words as she had of Captain Reynolds's. "I think we should have some lunch. Don't you?"

*　*　*

After Mrs Ruane silenced Captain Reynolds's protestations by completely ignoring them—as seemed to be her way when faced with a question she had no interest in answering—she guided them inside.

The interior of the house did not disappoint Qi's imagination.

Mrs Ruane would not permit the guards to enter the house, but permitted Reynolds to keep his gun readied as long as he did not draw it. The staff, as numerous as Qi had expected they would be, handed out refreshments.

So within a few hours of crashing down and being arrested on suspicion of banditry, they were sipping fruit juice in a cool wide lounge filled with expensive furniture, with walls that featured a selection of severe-looking ancestors, many with the red hair Mrs Ruane displayed.

It was like attending a party in a place you didn't know and with too few people to allow casual chit-chat.

Mrs Ruane appeared at Qi's side, took her left hand and tucked it under her right arm. She seemed utterly unconcerned at her familiarity. "Come along with me, Captain."

She led Qi through double doors and along a corridor to a much smaller sitting room. Mrs Ruane released Qi's hand, threw herself into an armchair and let out a long sigh.

"I am so sorry about the imposition of you having to come here with Captain Reynolds," she said. "But perhaps it is not all bad."

Qi perched on the edge of an armchair facing her. She was not entirely familiar with appropriate behaviour in the British upper classes, but she was quite certain that Mrs Ruane was not exhibiting it.

"I understand you've been having trouble with bandits."

"Yes. And that's why your arrival is so fortuitous."

"It is?"

"Of course. Now that you're here you'll be able to carry an attack party into the mountains so we can rout the bandits once and for all."

7

Terry leaned on the wooden railing of the upper deck. Next to him, the Frenchman smoked a cigarette while Ichiro stared off into the distance. It was not that Ichiro was hard to read. Terry had met Japanese before and while they were like closed books, if Ichiro were a book he would be one for children, with pictures and colour plates.

It was because of his deafness; every movement he made was huge, and he liked it when people were that way to him. Ichiro focused and turned his head, his grin spreading across his face as he realised Terry was staring at him.

We work now. Ichiro's hands flicked in quick embrasive movements. The boy loved to work. Terry held up his hand to indicate *not yet* as he nodded at the four British soldiers who also watched the departing group.

Terry wondered how scared they were. Well, it was up to him to put them at their ease. The Frenchman could irritate a Buddhist without raising a sweat, and they had no chance of understanding Ichiro.

He climbed over the railing and made his way down the ladder. One of the soldiers brought up his gun. Once he had reached halfway Terry jumped down to the rocky river bed.

"You boys want a drink?" All four of them were Indian: one of them a corporal by his stripes, the others privates.

"We don't drink."

"I was thinking tea, mate," Terry said with a smile. "Don't touch the sauce myself. The froggy only drinks wine or one of his fancy French liqueurs."

They looked at the corporal for guidance.

"They're going to be gone a long time, right? Back tomorrow at the earliest so we better get settled and get to know one another. Right?"

They relaxed a little. Terry smiled and stuck out his hand. "Terry Montgomery, late of Adelaide, Australia."

The corporal slung his rifle over his shoulder and shook. "Corporal Rajagopal." The soldier glanced up at the other two.

Terry leaned in a little. "Frenchie's name is Remy Darras, aggravating bastard but a genius with the balloons. Just don't tell him I said that." The corporal grinned. "And the big guy is Ichiro, but he can't hear a word, he's a gentle giant. Don't let him hug you, he'll crush your ribs."

All four soldiers were now relaxed and smiling, looking up at Remy and Ichiro. Terry allowed himself a relaxed smile. At least nobody was going to get shot, as long as Remy kept his sarcastic comments to himself.

* * *

The tea had gone down well, even with tinned milk. You got used to it. Only the bridge would have been big enough to hold them all— the ship's mess was only good for four at one time—but Terry didn't think the captain would appreciate it.

So he had Ichiro set up a table and chairs from around the ship in the cargo bay close to the open doors. Remy had not joined them. He had sniffed at the idea of tea and had gone up top to fiddle with the balloon gear while they waited for supplies to do his repairs.

"So how long does it take to get to—what? Your barracks?"

The corporal nodded. "By the Big House, two hours from here."

"That's quite some artillery piece you boys have got."

"Not really, Mr Montgomery. It may be big but I think you know it is quite old. I think perhaps you are being deceiving."

Terry tensed. He'd kept his sleeves rolled down to hide his tattoos. "Why would you say that?"

"You are a military man. This much is clear."

Terry forced a smile onto his face. Lying was against the Fourth Precept.

"I was. It was another life," he said. "I moved on."

The corporal looked as if he wanted to say something else but thought better of it and stood up. "We need to arrange patrols."

The other three soldiers rose, brushed themselves down and straightened their uniforms.

"It's not safe here then?"

"This is one of the valleys the bandits use when they raid."

"And they attack the main house this way?"

The corporal shook his head. "They take from the peasants."

One aspect of never lying was that it became much easier to tell when someone else was not being entirely truthful. But Terry did not think it wise to push the point.

"All right, mate, well we'll get back to our work then. Good getting to know you."

The soldiers left the cargo hold and Terry watched the corporal giving his orders pointing up the valley and round. They set off in two groups of two, the corporal leading the first; when they were a hundred paces away the second pair followed. Weapons at the ready.

Ichiro was gathering up the chairs.

Leave them, signed Terry. *We'll want them here later.* He knew his ability with signing didn't quite communicate exactly what he was thinking in his head, but Ichiro was good at interpreting what people meant.

He might be big, but he was no one's fool.

They make you sad, Ichiro signed and placed his hand on Terry's arm.

Terry shook his head and gently pulled his arm free.

The sun was still high. They had managed to kill a couple of hours, but the monotony was going to kick in pretty soon. Better to keep busy. The galley could do with a thorough clean and sort out; that Cameron woman kept putting things back in the wrong place.

Terry came awake at the sound of a gunshot and threw himself out of his bunk. Moonlight was filtering through the porthole, not bright but enough to let him make out the shapes and shadows.

Terry slept half-dressed from habit, so he grabbed an old sweater, a shade darker than his skin, and pulled it over his head. He stopped and listened. Ichiro was snoring in the berth next door. He hadn't heard anything, of course.

Another shot rang out and echoed back from the mountains. A rifle, close by. Probably one of the army boys. Last thing he knew they'd been arranging to keep patrols on the top deck, with the cargo doors locked shut. It was a good enough plan, as there was little cover close to the ship.

He opened his door and went out into the almost-black of the companionway, as he knew the ship's layout intimately and needed no light. He opened Ichiro's door and stepped through. Ichiro's room was as sparsely furnished as his own. Possessions were a trap.

He shook Ichiro's arm and the big man grabbed his wrist, immobilising it. In the half-light Terry pressed his finger to his lips and saw the grin spread over Ichiro's face. Terry frowned. It was not a stupid sign to make; Ichiro needed to know that he should avoid making a sound.

Not that he'd know if he did.

Terry pointed at the porthole and then made stabbing signs into his hand. He had no idea how to express the concept of "bandits." Ichiro lost his grin, and made the same moves as if to clarify them. Terry nodded, keeping eye contact to ensure Ichiro realised the seriousness of the situation.

He moved to the door and gestured for Ichiro to follow.

"Monsieur Montgomery, *ou es tu?*" Remy's hiss pierced the silence of the corridor.

Terry moved out into the passage.

"Is it you?" asked Remy.

"Well, if it wasn't, you'd be dead by now," Terry muttered.

"When I have a gun and you do not, I do not think that would be the case."

"Quiet. Follow me."

"*Bien sur.*"

Terry glanced heavenwards in a quick prayer to whoever might be there to silence the Frenchman, who seemed to have little grasp of the concept of "quiet."

They moved through the ship until they reached a ladder up to a hatch in the top deck. He could see the stars through the opening. There had been silence since the last gunshot. Terry gestured for the other two to remain where they were, and he climbed until his head was just below the level of the open trapdoor.

"Hisssst," he said quietly. There was sound of something rubbing against the wood of the upper deck.

"Name?"

"Montgomery, what's my first name?"

There was a moment's hesitation. "Terry."

"Advance, friend."

The head of the corporal appeared, silhouetted against the stars.

"We have bandits." It wasn't a question.

"There appear to be. One of my men is wounded."

"How many are there and which way?"

"Number unknown but they have not rushed us so I do not expect many. We saw them moving by the river."

Terry digested the information recalling what he could of the terrain, the edge on which they were perched, the river and the valley.

"Give me three minutes and then open fire. Keep them busy for five minutes, then don't fire unless they rush the ship."

"Very good, I understand."

His head moved out of sight. Terry contemplated for a moment how refreshing it was to deal with trained personnel instead of civilians all the time. Then he climbed down into the ship.

"Give me your gun, Remy."

"You do not use guns."

"I hope to keep it that way." Terry held out his hand and Remy handed over the revolver. "Let's just hope they haven't put any more holes in the balloons."

"*Sacre*, I hope not."

"If you can think of anything to help protect the ship, do it. Otherwise stay out of the line of fire."

"Do not worry, *mon ami*, my life is very precious to me."

If Ichiro was upset at not being able to follow what they were saying, he did not show it. He simply stood, waiting.

Terry touched Ichiro's arm and indicated for him to follow. They went through to the bridge and then took the stairs down into the hold. Terry did not dare light the electrics. While it was true the hold was well sealed to keep the cold in for the ice cargo, he did not know whether light would show through anywhere.

They reached the small hatch in the main cargo door at the front of the ship, furthest from the action. Unless, of course, the bandits were planning the same thing as he—in which case this might be a very short and ineffectual military action.

As slowly as possible, to avoid any noise, he unbolted the door. He pulled it open and peered out. The moon's position placed this side of the ship in blackest shadow. Both good and bad. It would hide his exit, but prevented him from seeing if anyone else was there.

The fields were laid out in the silver light, looking calm and quiet. The gunfire would have echoed across the whole valley, but no peasant would take an interest. They preferred not to get involved. Terry understood that completely.

He stepped into the cold outside air. Ichiro followed. Terry stopped immediately, laid his hand on the man's chest and pushed him back. Ichiro made a small noise. Terry cringed, but the river splashing over the edge and into the valley would hide any small sounds.

Or so he told himself.

He found Ichiro's hand and pressed that to Ichiro's chest and then forced his arm back towards the door. He manipulated his fingers in the dark so the big man's hand was pointing, and made it move towards the door.

Ichiro extricated his fingers from Terry's and laid his hand on Terry's shoulder, then gently pushed him away. Terry took a few steps. Ichiro did not follow; his shadow merged with the ship, and the door closed.

Another gunshot rang out, followed by a fusillade. Terry heaved a sigh of relief and, crouching low, headed for where the river disappeared over the edge.

9

As Terry expected, the edge was not an abrupt cutoff where the ground suddenly fell away into oblivion. Instead it was rough, with various levels where the river water had eroded gently curving rocks and other places where whole chunks had fallen away, leaving deep grooves with flat bottoms.

It was not too difficult clambering along the precipice keeping his head below ground level, but it was wet and cold. His hands began to grow numb as he descended into another cut, clinging to grasses and reeds that were generally well rooted but occasionally gave way in a heart-stopping jerk.

Eventually he passed the water flow and reached the other bank. In the wet season even this would be flooding with water, but not now. It also meant that he was more aware of any noise he made. He clambered a distance further and then moved up towards ground level.

Sporadic firing still burst from the dark shadow of the ship on his left. The soldiers were moving between shots to prevent being targeted by the muzzle flashes.

The return fire was coming from a position almost directly up the valley from him. The soldiers would stop firing soon; that would mean the bandits' attention would begin to wander. He needed to move faster.

Fortune favoured the brave, or so he'd heard. He crouched low and moved at a fast walk, not directly towards the bandits but at an angle to take him closer but further behind them. Only a minute had passed when he noticed that the firing from the *Beauty* had stopped.

One or two shots rang out from the bandits, and then it all went silent.

He stopped moving and hunkered down, trying to blend into the shadows.

If the bandits were intelligent they might guess the firing was cover. He hoped it did not occur to them. He fingered the gun in his pocket. He should have removed the bullets; there was always the chance he might hurt someone, even kill them. It wasn't good playing games with a loaded gun.

He would have heaved a sigh, but that would have been too noisy.

Moving like a snake, he wound his way across the ground, approaching the group of bandits. They had been spread out when shooting but now that it was quiet they moved together. So much the better. They were probably wondering what to do next. The ship was clearly well defended, so what did they think they would gain by storming it?

Perhaps they thought it carried some valuable cargo. They would be sorely disappointed. It wasn't that the cargo wasn't valuable, but if it wasn't kept cool it wouldn't survive. There was some leeway for delivery but not a great deal.

How much risk were the bandits willing to take? And how soon?

Minutes passed and Terry wormed his way closer. The sound of running water filled his ears and he realized he was moving through the edges of the river water again. The sound would still help to protect him; he just did not like getting wet.

He was no more than a hundred yards away when their voices drifted past him, intermingled with the splashing of the river. They were talking in one of the native languages, of which there were hundreds; it could be any one of them. He had not expected to be able understand them. He just hoped they would understand him. They would probably understand the gun, regardless.

Brilliant white light flooded the valley, pouring from three of the *Beauty*'s spotlights. Terry blinked. Those lights were not designed to run from the batteries, and only to last a short time. Remy had been busy.

The bandits were blinking and shielding their eyes.

Terry pushed himself to his feet. His muscles ached from the unusual exercise but he ignored the pain. As fast as he could, he covered the intervening distance. Remy had taken a big risk; he might have been much further away and unable to take advantage.

"Put your hands up or I will shoot you dead!" he shouted.

The blinking bandits turned in surprise. Three of the seven raised their guns; they were now facing away from the lights, unlike him. Terry fired at the ground between them. His stomach churned from the false feeling of power the gun gave him. He hated it.

The warning shot had the desired effect. They all raised their hands into the air, just as the spotlights dimmed.

Terry fired again just to make a point, to ensure they did not think the dimming was a cue to go on the offensive.

"Put down your guns!"

At least two of them spoke English because they crouched to place their weapons on the ground. Looking at them in the dying light Terry got the feeling they were looking over his shoulder.

At something behind him.

He spun round. Another bandit loomed out of the dark, brandishing a sword. Terry ducked as the weapon sliced over his head. The temptation of the gun filled Terry. All he had to do was shoot the man.

He did not want to die, though he knew death was only a temporary affair. He fought his military training that would simply raise the gun and shoot his opponent dead. He dodged again, and slipped on a wet stone. As he went down he heard his attacker cry out.

He looked up and saw his opponent rise into the air, his legs dangling and jerking ineffectually. A look of terror contorted the man's face. As if he were nothing but a child's rag doll, he was tossed to the side and crashed to the ground, striking his head.

Ichiro loomed out of the dark, grinning, and pointed behind Terry. He turned quickly and fired once more as the bandits made to run.

"Stay right where you are."

10

There were songbirds in her dream. Very loud songbirds. Qi tried to shoo them away so they would not wake her up.

Did that mean she was still asleep?

She thought about it. No. She wasn't asleep. And the songbirds were still very loud. But the bed was extraordinarily comfortable. She lay face down on a spring mattress that supported her weight evenly, layers of finely woven cotton both beneath her and draped across her body.

Mrs Ruane. The house. The soldiers. The storm. The ship. *Beauty!*

She pushed herself up, she was wearing a cotton nightgown with blue bows that had been laid out on the bed in her room. She usually slept in her underwear when they were on the ground. When they were in the air she might catch a few minutes in her bunk, fully dressed.

There was no one else about. She looked at her wrist and remembered she'd removed her watch along with everything else. It had been a novelty. A clock on the mantel told her it was a quarter past six.

Water splashed somewhere nearby and the combined scents of oranges and roses floated through the room. Qi sat back on her heels in the middle of the bed as a female servant came in, bowed her head and pressed her palms together. "Your bath is ready, *sahiba*."

* * *

Qi had almost kicked up a fuss over the bath and the bathing. It was not that she was shy about her body—even though the nuns had tried to turn their pupils into prudes—but she was perfectly capable of both washing and drying herself. The maid's help was not required.

But she did accept the maid's assistance with her hair. Some of the younger nuns had, from time to time, enjoyed brushing the girls' hair, and that was one service Qi was willing to accept. The maid also oiled it and knotted it into a tight, thick plait down her back.

However, while she was happy that her leather trousers, jacket, and linen shirt had all been returned spotlessly clean—and the leather had been oiled—she was less than happy that her heavy-duty underthings were nowhere to be found, having been replaced by flimsy items that were unlikely to last a day.

The maid became so distraught at Qi's anger that the captain was completely unable to maintain it. She gave up, put on the lightweight replacements and wrapped herself in her leather armour, against the world.

*   *   *

If Mrs Ruane had been waiting for Qi to leave her room, she managed to make it look as if she had simply been passing at a fortuitous moment. Then again, perhaps it really had been coincidence.

The tall woman was wearing a dress that simultaneously catered to British tastes in corsetry while not being too heavy, so allowing the wearer some relief from the heat. It might have been argued that the extremely revealing décolletage served the same cooling purpose. However, Qi imagined it would have quite the opposite effect on any male viewer.

"Captain Qi, good morning."

Something about her Irish accent mixed with her throaty voice made it seem that she was perpetually flirting with whomever she spoke to.

"Mrs Ruane," said Qi. "I must thank you for your kind hospitality."

"You are guests, like shipwrecked sailors. What else would I do for someone in need?"

"We can't repay your kindness."

Mrs Ruane smiled. "Have you considered what I said last night?"

Qi pursed her lips. She'd walked straight into that trap. Damn those bloody nuns for their lessons in politeness.

"Let's go down to breakfast, shall we?"

She stepped past the captain, closer than she needed to. Her hand lingered a moment, and her fingertips brushed across the back of Qi's hand.

Qi could not decide whether Mrs Ruane's behaviour was because the lady was genuinely attracted to her, or because the lady thought she might add to the persuasion by promising her a night of passion. It was not something Qi was interested in, either way. And she did not like being manipulated.

Mrs Ruane paused at the top of the sweeping staircase. "Are you coming?"

Qi set off after her.

*　*　*

The captain almost failed to recognise Fanning, who was looking cleaner than Qi had ever seen. Mrs Cameron looked the same as she ever did while Otto's suit was pristine. Qi looked again, no, it was a new suit and his shoes had been buffed to a brilliant shine. But Otto was not looking at the captain. He—along with an almost drooling Fanning and, once again, Mrs Cameron—had fixed his gaze on their hostess.

Qi frowned. Was she the only person immune to this woman's charms?

Food was set out on tables round the edge of the room with servants ready to serve it up. Mrs Ruane collected a plate and went round, making her selections. The rest of the company followed her lead.

"Apparently taking one's breakfast in this fashion is all the rage back in England and Ireland," said Mrs Ruane. "It's much more relaxed, don't you think?"

The last time Qi had had a formal breakfast of any sort, as far as she could recall, had been at least seven years earlier. "We normally just take turns in the mess."

Mrs Ruane laughed. "The mess?"

"Our"—Qi searched for a way to describe the pokey little space—"dining room. It's not very big. There's not much formality on small boats."

Mrs Ruane sat down and tucked into the impressive stack on her plate. Mrs Cameron had selected a delicate amount, while Fanning and Otto had enormous piles of food.

"I look forward to being given a tour."

Qi was in the middle of choosing a breakfast somewhat more significant than Mrs Cameron's while not being as greedy as the others when a servant came to the door.

"Captain Reynolds, Madam."

The Captain strode in, clean and polished. He nodded at Qi then bowed to the mistress of the house.

"Have some breakfast, Captain."

"I'm afraid we must be moving out. I have received word that there were shots fired in the vicinity of the crashed ship."

"Shots?" Qi put down her plate of untouched food. She looked at Mrs Ruane. "We have to go, now." She addressed the captain again. "If my crew is harmed I shall hold you personally responsible, Captain Reynolds."

He touched his helmet. "Captain Qi, I am as concerned as you. I will be riding out with a small detachment. They are saddling up."

"I want to come with you."

"Can you ride?"

"I can manage."

11

"I'm afraid Mrs Ruane has upset your plans to treat us like common criminals," said Qi as conversationally as was feasible on horseback, trotting along the muddy path.

She and Captain Reynolds were flanked by ten Sikh soldiers carrying wicked-looking swords along with their rifles. All ten sported impressive moustaches and beards. They had already covered a third of the distance and were approaching the turn in the road where it met the main valley. It had been difficult to convince Dingbang to remain at the house; in the end she ordered him to remain since they could not leave Otto and Fanning.

"Mrs Ruane is a law unto herself," said Captain Reynolds, his voice tight and resigned. "However you are not off the hook as far as I am concerned, Captain."

"I really think we got off on the wrong foot."

"I have nothing against you personally, Captain Qi. You seem a decent person, for a Chinese."

For a moment Qi lost the rhythm of the gait and was roughly bumped around—she did not use the rising trot that the soldiers employed. "Shall we hurry?" she said to avoid making a caustic comment and kicked her horse into a canter.

She pulled away for a moment but Reynolds's mount shifted up a gear and soon drew alongside. He was riding a stallion that was probably higher up the pecking order than the smaller mare they'd given her.

"I am afraid I insulted you," said Reynolds.

"Never mind, Captain. I assure you I am quite used to your British prejudices."

"I believe I am trying to apologise."

"Relationships between our nations have never been easy and, in case you'd forgotten, you invaded us."

"Are you suggesting we should not have helped put down the Boxer Rebellion?"

"Captain, you have no idea what went on," she said through gritted teeth. "If you did you would not discuss it so casually."

Mercifully her comment managed to shut him up. She was not foolish enough to believe every story that was told about the depredations on the allied forces that had landed in China to deal with the Boxers. But even if only a fraction of those stories were true, the British and their European allies had no right to make any comment.

After ten minutes they dropped back into a trot. They were now moving along the valley with the fields to their right and the agricultural terraces to their left.

When she was very young Qi had spent a couple of years working in the rice fields up to her calves in water, planting and harvesting. The nuns had provided some relief from the interminable work with their school. Not all children were allowed to attend but her father had given her uncle strict instructions that she was to be educated. So she was.

"The guards are not where they should be," said Captain Reynolds as they reached the head of the valley. He was examining the area with a spyglass. She was relieved to see the *Beauty* still sitting where she'd left it. Not that it could have flown away, but there was always the risk someone might set fire to it. "You should keep back while we go in."

"I'll be going with you, Captain. It's my ship and my men."

He acquiesced with a nod.

They dismounted. Four of the guards went on ahead while Qi, Captain Reynolds and the remainder walked openly forward in a loose group.

* * *

Terry Montgomery was busy pushing a rag on the end of a broom handle into a pipe to clean it when the piercing whistle of the communication tube blew. He lifted it off its hook and put it to his ear though he knew no one would speak. Three urgent whistles sounded—Ichiro's signal.

He left the cleaning and hurried up to the top deck. Remy was ignoring the action, still checking the balloon envelopes for bullet holes after the events of the previous night. He had started at daybreak and would have begun earlier if he had been able to see in the dark. He muttered and fussed in French as he went through the cloth an arm's-length at a time.

Looking out across the green landscape Terry spotted the four advance guards making their way around the perimeter and nodded in approval. The approaching group, having noticed the missing soldiers, was now taking appropriate steps in case of trouble. Ichiro handed Terry the telescope and he trained it on the mounted group. Captain Qi was among them. Good.

He handed the telescope back to Ichiro and signed *keep watch,* then crossed to the other side of the ship. One of the Indian soldiers stood there with his gun trained on the bandits below, while a second stood a short distance away. Montgomery leaned his elbow on the railing.

"Your captain is on the way back. Must have got word of the shooting last night. You might want to make yourselves known before they open fire."

The man nodded and shouted down to the other in one of the Indian languages that Terry vaguely recognised. The soldier below waved and headed round the ship towards the drop-off into the valley.

The bandits weren't very bright and, as their guard moved away, they wriggled around testing the knots. The man standing beside Terry cocked his weapon noisily. That was enough to cause an immediate cessation of motion and several worried glances in their direction. Terry gave them a pleasant wave.

* * *

They were on the bridge, and Qi watched as Captain Reynolds shook Terry's hand. "Thank you."

Terry nodded and accepted the thanks. "I did it for the ship."

"Well, I'm still grateful," said the captain. He held on to Terry's hand a little longer than would be expected, looking at the tattoos on his arm. "Fusiliers?"

Terry jerked back his hand. "Sorry, I was in the middle of cleaning the engine."

"Captain Reynolds," said Qi. "Have we earned your trust yet?"

The captain watched Terry disappear through the hatch into the depths of the ship. "As he said, he did it for the ship. Not for us."

"What are you going to do with the bandits?"

"Take them back and interrogate them. See if they know anything useful."

Qi thought about trying to persuade him to let her stay, but she couldn't do anything useful here nor could she leave the other crewmembers in the clutches of Mrs Ruane.

"We'd better be going, then."

12

They arrived back late afternoon. The bandits did not walk with much enthusiasm, even with Sikh swords at their backs. Qi thought perhaps if the soldiers had used those swords once or twice it might have encouraged them to go faster. But Captain Reynolds felt there were certain proprieties to be followed, and those included no unnecessary violence to prisoners.

"After all," he said when she suggested it, "we have no proof as yet that they are bandits."

"They attacked my ship."

Apparently this was not sufficient.

Mrs Ruane was delighted to see her and gave her a hug that lasted considerably longer than such a greeting warranted—assuming a hug was an appropriate greeting in the first instance.

After the evening meal Qi watched as Mrs Cameron, Otto, Fanning and Mrs Ruane played croquet on the lawn. They seemed to be enjoying themselves, though only Mrs Cameron was holding her own against their host. Every now and then Dingbang would appear between flowerbeds, wandering through the gardens accompanied by one of Mrs Ruane's gardeners, studying the plants. Occasionally he would crouch down to examine one more closely. Qi had known him for most of her life and had had no idea he was interested in plants.

Qi, on the other hand, sat doing nothing and itching for action. She wanted the moving ship under her feet, the feeling of lightness the Faraday gave them; she even wanted the mountains and the ice. She did not think she had ever been this idle before in her life, even when she was a child. But she forced herself to remain in the chair, shaded by a parasol and leaning on a table, with a constant supply of water in the jug by her side.

To think every single one of Mrs Ruane's days was like this. No wonder she fed off the life of her guests.

Captain Reynolds was announced. He emerged from the house and descended the stone steps to the lawn. He came up beside her and watched the game for several minutes, seemingly as unhurried as their host.

"Your crew are not skilled in this game," he commented, without malice.

"No," she said.

Mrs Ruane glanced over at them from across the lawn. She nodded to the captain and gave Qi a sly wink which the captain could not possibly have missed.

"Is there a Mr Ruane?" said Qi.

"There is such a man," said the captain. "But he is never here, and I believe that suits his wife."

"Yes, I am sure you are correct."

There was a long pause as the game continued.

"I have some good news," said the captain at length. "I have received confirmation regarding your ship, although Fanning and Mrs Cameron are not mentioned."

"Fanning is a recent addition and, as I said, Mrs Cameron has chartered the ship."

The captain cleared his throat. "There was, however, a note about a Mr Cameron in Delhi claiming his wife had been stolen away from him."

Qi did not reply but watched Mrs Cameron whack her ball firmly through a hoop and knock another ball away. Otto frowned.

"The name is an interesting coincidence," said Captain Reynolds. "Even the Christian name is the same. Beatrice."

"That certainly is an interesting coincidence," said Qi.

They were both silent for a moment. Beatrice Cameron laughed as Mrs Ruane's ball ricocheted off the hoop and sent hers spinning across the grass.

"However," said the captain, "this Beatrice Cameron is not in need of any rescue, therefore cannot be the same one."

Qi smiled. "So if we are not enemies of the British Empire does that mean we can leave?"

"Well, I am happy for you to start work on your ship as soon as your supplies are delivered."

"Thank you."

A cheer went up from the lawn as Mrs Cameron whacked her ball. It slammed into another one, careened off it and struck the final pin.

The group made their way up to the tables.

"I do not understand," Otto was saying. "I understand the mathematics and I was quite accurate in my striking of the ball but I did not succeed."

"You don't have the killer instinct," said Mrs Cameron.

"Killer instinct?"

"It's not just about hitting your ball accurately. It's about making sure the others don't win."

Captain Reynolds gave Qi a short bow, and took Mrs Ruane aside. As Qi watched he spoke to her quietly as he handed her an envelope. Mrs Ruane took the envelope as if it were poison and then moved away from the group. After a moment's indecision, she ripped it open and removed a single sheet.

As she scanned the letter her mood changed as if a cloud had passed over the sun. Stiffening, she looked up. She beckoned to the captain and said something to him, after which he immediately went into the house. Mrs Ruane glanced at her guests for a moment, and

Qi hastily averted her eyes to hide the fact she had been watching. Mrs Ruane followed the captain inside.

"I wonder what that's about," said Beatrice in a low voice close to Qi's ear.

"You noticed."

"Oh yes. I've sat across the breakfast table from someone getting bad news in a letter," she said. "And, if I am not much mistaken, that news was very grave indeed."

Qi assumed Beatrice was referring to her ne'er-do-well husband but decided it was not worth mentioning that her husband was looking for her. At least not yet.

* * *

It was late evening; the sun had gone down. There had been a late supper without Mrs Ruane, and the others had gone to bed. The need to feel the moving deck of the *Beauty* beneath her feet again kept Qi awake and restless, so she wandered the dark corridors of the quiet house.

She came down into the drawing room. Moonlight filtered through the window, dappling the walls and floor in silver and shadow. Qi found a stoppered carafe of water. The water glugged noisily into the glass and she replaced the stopper with a loud clink.

"Who's there?" said Mrs Ruane, from one of the high-backed chairs. Her voice wavered as if she had been crying. Her usual confident tone was missing.

"Qi Zang."

Mrs Ruane rose from her chair, which was facing away from where Qi stood. She did not turn but walked to the French window. She was in a silk dressing gown that clung and moved with her body. The moonlight gave it a silver sheen.

Qi picked up the glass. "Is there something wrong, Mrs Ruane?"

"Call me Kathleen."

Qi traced her way through the room and stood beside her host, looking out into the night-shrouded garden.

"How important is wallpaper, Captain Qi?" Kathleen's voice broke as if she were crying again.

Qi blinked in confusion. "I'm sorry?"

"Never mind."

There was a further period of silence.

"You saw that I received a letter."

"It did not contain pleasing news."

"It did not," agreed Mrs Ruane. "Someone I care about is being held for ransom by the bandits."

"I see."

"Captain, may I ask that you transport me to pay the ransom and recover my friend?"

Qi hesitated.

"I will pay for your repairs and a sum equal to the ransom if you can return my friend to me."

Qi still hesitated, as she did not wish to put her crew in harm's way—but even so she inquired. "How much is the ransom?"

"Five hundred pounds."

13

"Well, Monsieur Darras?"

Remy adjusted a valve on his torch and the bright flame reduced to a small blue light. He pushed up his goggles with his gauntleted hand. He was the most untidy she had ever seen him.

"Two hours to get the new piping in place, *Capitaine*."

"And the balloon envelope?"

Remy nodded to where Beatrice, Fanning and Ichiro were working on the cloth, replacing an area that had been burnt away by the lightning strike. "Perhaps a similar time. Then we must attach it and test it."

"Very good."

Qi walked across the top deck to the railing and looked down over the side. Captain Reynolds was there with a dozen of his men. Mrs Ruane stood apart from them, dressed in travelling clothes and staring out across the valley.

"I do not think Mrs Ruane has come to see us off," said Dingbang at her side. She had not noticed him arrive.

"No, she is coming with us."

"Into Kerala? To the Fortress?"

"We have a side job." Dingbang was silent so Qi continued. "It's five hundred pounds."

"That is a great deal of money."

"That's why I agreed."

"And what must we do for this money?"

"Rescue a woman from the bandits."

"We are traders, not fighters."

"We fight when we must, and besides," she said, "they will be the ones doing the fighting. We carry them to the rendezvous, show superior fire power and they get the woman back."

"I do not think this is wise, little one."

"Think of the money."

"I am thinking of your father."

Qi felt a burst of anger. "I am the captain."

Dingbang gave her a bow just on the wrong side of politeness and headed for the hatch. She frowned at his back.

* * *

The bridge was crowded. The expected crew were there, along with Beatrice, Fanning, Mrs Ruane, Captain Reynolds and one of his men to act as runner if he needed to communicate with the rest of his men in the cargo hold.

Steam pressure was up and the generators were running smoothly. Qi sounded the klaxon for the one-minute alert to engaging the Faraday. She caught herself stroking the helm and quickly looked to see if anyone had noticed. There were so many people around her, yet she had almost forgotten about them, so strong was the pleasure of being in command of the *Beauty* once more.

The chronometer clicked through another minute. It seemed as if the people on the bridge held their collective breath until she reached out and engaged the Faraday.

The lightness washed through her. She could feel *Beauty* straining to be aloft. She checked the wind gauge; there was a breeze running down the valley but that was no risk. It would only push them out across the valley, which was entirely acceptable. Using the communication pipe she gave Remy the order to complete inflating the envelopes. "Make your height 1000 feet, Monsieur Darras."

"Aye, *Capitaine*," came his tinny reply.

If they had been at an official air-dock the envelopes would have been tied down until given the command to release. But in this situation they would simply lift when the buoyancy exceeded their Faraday weight.

The stern lifted a fraction and the *Beauty* slid sedately across the river bed. The bow hit a boulder, and the ship turned. The view through the bridge viewing ports angled round until they were looking up the valley.

Qi smiled to herself. *Almost as if it were planned.* She sent the order to engage the main propeller and felt the familiar vibration as it spun up to speed. The river bed dropped away from them at an increasing rate.

"Oh my goodness," breathed Mrs Ruane from where she stood to the side of the window. She took a step backwards and grabbed at a pipe in the wall for balance.

Qi held back on the forward thrust to maintain their position against the breeze and allowed the ship to drift backwards until they could see where the river fell over the drop-off into the fields below.

"Course please, *Herr* Kröne."

"North by northwest, Captain," he shouted. "Along the valley."

The captain applied half thrust and moments later felt the *Beauty* push ahead, reaching perhaps fifteen knots against the headwind. Qi unhooked the communication tube again and whistled to Remy.

"Oui, *Capitaine*?"

"How are the repairs?"

"All good, *Capitaine*, but I would not wish to apply excessive pressure at this time."

"I'll keep things easy until you're happy."

"Merci."

Mrs Ruane turned from the bird's-eye view of the valley and took the few short steps to the helm.

"You have an excellent crew, Captain."

"I am very proud of them."

"Can we go up on top?" the older woman asked.

"Would you go with her, Dingbang?" He nodded. She returned her gaze to Mrs Ruane. "You must stay out of the way of Monsieur Darras, and follow the orders of my first mate."

Mrs Ruane raised an eyebrow. "His orders?"

For a moment Qi considered modifying her statement but caught the frown in Dingbang's face. "His orders, Kathleen. This is not a cruise ship. It is not designed for safety or, indeed, any passengers."

Mrs Ruane hesitated and then acknowledged with a nod of her head. "His orders."

"Would you like accompany them, Captain Reynolds?" Qi asked, hoping she could get all the passengers off her bridge.

"How long to the rendezvous?"

"Two hours I believe." She looked across to Otto.

"Two hours and twelve minutes under current conditions, Captain."

Qi turned to Captain Reynolds, who nodded. "Then I will accompany Mrs Ruane."

As the group left the bridge, Qi heaved a sigh of relief. She did not like strangers on her ship.

14

"We will not be going in with all your guns blazing, Captain Reynolds," said Qi.

"No indeed, Captain," said Mrs Ruane. "I do not want Miss Chabak harmed."

"She will not be harmed, as well you know, Mrs Ruane," muttered Captain Reynolds.

The three of them were hunched round the table in the small mess. Mrs Cameron had put together a light luncheon of sandwiches and coffee—which Qi found strangely incongruous considering the nature of their conversation. However, the captain's last remark piqued her interest.

"How is it we know they will not harm this woman?" she asked.

Mrs Ruane looked awkward. The captain stared at her pointedly.

"Because Dhavni Chabak is the sister of Kehar Chabak."

"And who is Kehar Chabak?"

"The bandit leader."

"He has kidnapped his own sister? That does not seem usual," said Qi. "What else have you not told me?"

Captain Reynolds gave Mrs Ruane another hard stare and rose to his feet. "If you would excuse me? I must see how my men are doing. Ladies." He pulled open the door as far as it would go and squeezed through the gap.

Qi looked expectantly at Mrs Ruane who, once more, seemed discomfited. After staring for a short time at her own hands clasped on the table, Qi took a drink from her glass of water.

"What is it that you are not telling me?" she asked again, as an afterthought in the hope it might get a better response. "Kathleen."

Mrs Ruane smiled humourlessly. "We had an argument."

For a moment Qi thought she might mean with the captain, but that did not make any sense. "You and this…Dhavni?"

"We are"—Mrs Ruane searched for the words—"romantically entwined."

Qi sighed. That explained some of Kathleen's behaviour. She looked up to see tears in the other woman's eyes. Qi did not carry a kerchief, nor was there anything suitable to hand. Kathleen sniffed.

"She did not like the wallpaper I had picked out for her room."

* * *

Back on the bridge, with the firm certainty of the *Beauty*'s helm in her grasp, Qi stared ahead at the mountains that loomed on either side of them. The valley they had been following was long gone, and they had crossed more than one ridge. If they had not had the charts they would be completely lost. The British Army's Ordnance Survey had mapped almost every inch of the sub-continent with the help of their flying machines.

"I am completely opposed to handing over money to this bandit," said Captain Reynolds. "It is contrary to the welfare of His Majesty's Empire and of its citizens."

They were not alone on the bridge but Dingbang was doing an excellent impression of a statue, staring through the window ahead, keeping an eye out for landmarks. Otto had the maps spread across the desk and was consulting his notes while pretending not to listen. The last Qi knew, Fanning and Beatrice were talking to Mrs Ruane on the upper deck.

"The welfare you are duty-bound to uphold."

"Of course."

"But Mrs Ruane wants her … companion returned to her."

"The desires of one woman do not outweigh the security of the Empire."

"I do not think the Empire will suffer much if one bandit gets five hundred pounds for his sister."

"It depends on what he plans to do with it."

Qi glanced at the captain. "I have no desire to take my crew into a firefight. We are traders, not soldiers."

"Your Mr Montgomery most certainly is."

"Was. He is a Buddhist now, he will not fight."

"And yet he captured the bandits who attacked your ship."

"I did not say he was not clever," she said. "And Ichiro helped."

Captain Reynolds fell silent but Qi could not let it rest. "I need to know what you're planning."

"The ship will be under the scrutiny of the bandits so I would like you to drop down early so my men and I can disembark while you make the rendezvous."

"All right," she said, grateful for the opportunity to get the soldiers off her ship. "Otto, how long to the rendezvous point?"

"Twenty minutes, Captain."

"Good," said Reynolds. "I will notify the men."

He strode away and headed through the door that led to the cargo bay. The door thudded shut behind him. Dingbang looked over at her and nodded. She thought she could see a slight smile creasing his face.

"Was that correct, Captain?" asked Otto with a slight uncertainty in his voice.

"That was perfect. Do you have a place where we can drop him off?"

"I found a location a few miles from the meeting point."

Dingbang looked round. "He has horses."

It was Otto's turn to smile. "Yes, but there is a ridge one thousand feet high that he must cross."

* * *

Qi leaned against the side of the cargo hold entrance, her arms crossed. Captain Reynolds and his men had spent a few minutes settling their horses after the ship had landed. The animals seemed none the worse for their period in low gravity.

The men mounted up. Qi walked down the ramp and up to the captain's horse, which jostled left and right looking as if it were keen to be on the move. Around them the mountains reared up.

"The meeting place is three miles distant," said Qi, pointing at where the river-cut valley turned up into a higher one. "We saw a trail running alongside the river, so you should be able to make good time."

"Keep them busy for as long as you can," said the captain. "We should be with you in under an hour." He urged his horse forwards. The others fell in behind, and they moved off at a walk which turned into a slow trot.

Qi gave him a wave when he looked back, then turned on her heel and marched back inside. Ichiro grabbed the winding handle and the clattering of the ratchet accompanied the closing of the hatch.

Terry was standing just inside the hold. Qi paused as she approached. "They did just as you said they would. Thank you." He nodded and headed back towards the engine room.

Back on the bridge Qi engaged the Faraday and the *Beauty* floated upwards.

The instructions she had given the captain were not inaccurate; he would certainly have been suspicious if the *Beauty* did not fly past them and head up the valley itself. She watched as the horses grew closer and then disappeared behind.

"Make our height one thousand, Monsieur Darras," she said into the tube.

"Oui, *Capitaine.*"

The ship approached the ridge that rose up like a wall in front of them. Qi noted that the trail did cross the ridge, but it looked as if it would barely allow a man let alone a horse to travel it. They would have to dismount and lead their horses.

As they drew closer she killed their forward motion and guided the *Beauty* in towards the mountainside. It was delicate work as random gusts buffeted the ship. The last thing they needed was to tear the envelope again. Remy had been very unhappy about this part of the plan.

There was no way for Qi to see what was happening to the side of the ship, but Dingbang was at the portside portholes while Qi fought the winds to keep the ship as close to the cliff as possible, and above the trail.

"He is ready," announced Dingbang. Qi adjusted the thrusters to take them towards the mountain. The ship shuddered as the hull crashed into the rock. "He's away."

Gratefully Qi gunned the thrusters and pulled away, none too soon as a vicious down-draught cost them fifty feet of altitude in half a second. Qi took the ship directly away from the cliff face as she ordered Remy to give them two thousand feet of altitude. He swore down the line in French as the *Beauty* bounded skywards.

Qi brought the ship round in a full turn and saw Terry waving from the path. She estimated he had about two hundred feet to make the top of the ridge plus whatever it took to get down the other side. Unlike the captain and his men, Terry would be inconspicuous.

She reduced the engine power as they slipped over the ridge. The sun shone on them until she gave instructions for the descent and they dropped into shadow.

"The meeting place is here, Captain," said Otto.

She looked forward. The ridge fell away less precipitously on this side. There was a lake; a few scrawny trees lived on its banks along with a scattering of stubby bushes.

"There," said Dingbang. There was a line of smoke from a fire that looked to be at the far end of the lake. Near to the smoke were several horses.

Qi brought the *Beauty* low across the lake, following the shoreline, but carefully steered away from the trees and bushes from which the smoke emerged. The horses were, in fact, sturdy, long-haired ponies, saddled and ready to go.

She wasted time heading along the river and then back in a wide arc, finally setting down a good half mile from the fire. Once again she did not want to risk a bullet hole in the envelope. They could probably manage to fly with just a hole or two, since the ship could easily heat more air to fill the balloons, but they couldn't afford to suffer too many hits.

Better to keep the ship out of harm's way.

"Do you have the money?" Qi asked Mrs Ruane as they buckled on their coats. Qi felt awkward putting on her father's tatty old over-sized coat while her passenger donned her expensive and elegant attire. It was not a feeling that Qi experienced when with just her crew.

Mrs Ruane pulled a fat envelope from her large reticule—which by itself was probably worth ten pounds—and then replaced it.

Qi held out her hand for the envelope. "You should stay here."

"No, I am coming," said Mrs Ruane as she snapped the clasp on her bag.

"It won't be safe."

Mrs Ruane looked at Otto, Dingbang and Ichiro who were also getting ready. Only Ichiro was not armed, but he looked as if he could stop a charging bear. Fanning had complained about being left behind until Qi had pointed out that she needed someone who was willing to use force to protect Beatrice. At that Terry had raised an eyebrow but made no comment.

"I'll be safe," said Mrs Ruane.

"If it goes wrong, there will be shooting."

"Why would there be shooting? He has not kidnapped her, she went willingly."

"And now there is a ransom demand."

"It's her brother."

"Who is a bandit."

"Blood is thicker than water, Captain."

Qi pursed her lips but made no further argument. There was clearly something odd about this arrangement. If this Dhavni Chabak was willing to come home, why had she not simply done so? If she was going along with the ransom plan, did she really want to return to Kathleen? Qi shook her head. She was not planning on getting shot, and if that meant getting in her retribution first, so be it.

Mrs Ruane shivered as a cold wind cut through her coat when she stepped onto the valley floor. For Qi it was nothing compared to the temperatures they tolerated when cutting ice, so she barely noticed.

The party set off across the stony landscape with the lake on their right.

Qi and Mrs Ruane took the lead with the other three a short distance behind. Terry had suggested it would be best if they were to spread out. It would give them better firing lines and make it harder for someone to pick them off. Taking so many was also part of Qi's plan since more targets meant less concentrated fire on each.

Her breath steamed a little but was torn away by the cold wind flowing down from the mountains around them and along the valley floor.

They had covered more than half of the distance. Qi checked her watch. She estimated Captain Reynolds would take at least three hours to breach the ridge. There was no question that he would pursue his mission.

He was going to be very angry, so being finished before he arrived would be best.

There was no sign of anyone. She checked her gun and glanced back at the others. She did not know whether Otto was a good shot but he had handled the weapon well enough when he took it. He wasn't scared of it. She knew Dingbang could shoot, but it was not as if they had much practice when all they did was cut and haul ice.

They were a dozen yards from the first bush when a bullet ricocheted from the rocks in front of them. Seconds later the sound of its firing echoed round the rocks. They froze.

Though the temptation was strong Qi resisted her desire to try to find the sniper in the rocks. Terry had been right again. She kept her eyes on the undergrowth in front of them.

There was movement and two figures emerged: a man and a woman. Qi and her party had counted five horses when they descended so there were at least two more men in the bushes, possibly more.

Both were dressed in *salwar kameez*, though hers was both of better quality and in worse condition.

"Dhavni," said Mrs Ruane and started to move forward. Qi grabbed her arm. Dhavni did not move but her eyes were fixed on Mrs Ruane.

"*Sat Shri Akal,*" said the man, and nodded his head.

"You are Kehar Chabak?" said Qi.

"At your service." He gave an expansive and mocking bow. "And you are being?"

"Captain Qi Zang of the *Frozen Beauty*," she said. "And Mrs Ruane's escort."

"I greet you, Captain Qi Zang." He smiled. "You have my gift?"

Mrs Ruane shifted the bag in her hands. "Five hundred pounds sterling."

"A princely gift. You are doing me great honour."

"You are a coward and a criminal," shouted Mrs Ruane. Qi did not try to hush her; they needed to give Terry as much time as possible. "Dhavni, come to me."

The woman, perhaps five years younger than her brother, did not move. Her expression was pained.

"Dhavni, why do you not come to me?"

Kehal took a step forwards. "Because she is knowing her place as woman. She is thinking what I am telling her to think. She is doing what I tell her to do!"

From the angry expression on the young woman's face, now that her brother was in front of her instead of beside her, Qi deduced she did not agree with him. So, though she had run to him, she was not happy. Qi's concern about how this would play out increased. She was glad they had prepared.

"How shall we proceed?" asked Qi, attempting to defuse the immediate situation.

"What are you meaning *proceed*?" he said.

"With the exchange."

His laugh dripped condescension. "Exchange? There is no exchange. You are giving me money now."

16

Mrs Ruane made a sound that was somewhere between a growl and a sob. Qi glanced at her to ensure she was not about to do something they all might regret, but she stood firm.

A glance over her shoulder told her that the others remained where they were. Otto looked worried. It occurred to her that Ichiro had no idea what was happening. He wouldn't hear any gunshots, she cursed herself for a moment for being so stupid. Still, he was paying attention.

Her attention was caught by Kehar saying something to his sister. She refused whatever it was he had told her to do and he slapped her across the face.

Mrs Ruane took a step forward.

Barely had Qi had time to draw a breath than another bullet ricocheted in front of Mrs Ruane, followed by the report echoing through the rocks. Mrs Ruane froze. Qi sighed. Terry had not intercepted the sniper. This was not good.

"What are you going to do with her?" demanded Mrs Ruane.

Kehar ignored her and grabbed Dhavni by the wrist, twisting it. He gave his sister the same order as before, and pointed at Mrs Ruane. Qi guessed he was threatening to have her shot if Dhavni did not do as she was told.

The woman said something in a tone that was oddly both angry and acquiescent. She shook her wrist free of his grip and walked across to Mrs Ruane.

The two of them stood facing one another. Mrs Ruane towered over her, her red hair and pale skin contrasting with Dhavni's dark features and black hair. Neither of them said anything.

Mrs Ruane opened her bag and pulled out the envelope. As she passed it to Dhavni their fingers touched. For a moment they remained motionless as if life passed between them through this lightest of touches. Then Dhavni took the envelope and turned away. She walked back to her brother clutching the packet to her chest, one hand over the other.

Two rifle shots in quick succession echoed around the cliffs. But no bullets struck home. Terry's signal. It was a shame he had sworn off violence, as he was now in the perfect position to turn this to their advantage.

If wishes were horses, Qi thought to herself as she pulled out her gun and fired into the bushes. There was a cry of pain and the sound of a gun clattering to the ground. Kehar stared at Qi in horror for a moment then drew his gun and pointed it at his sister's stomach.

"No!" cried Mrs Ruane.

"Be staying back!" he shouted.

There was the crack of another pistol. Qi threw herself at Mrs Ruane and dragged her to the ground. They had no cover. She saw a shape lumbering past them and realised the gunshot had not been aimed at her. Ichiro did not realise he was being shot at, which gave him the appearance of insane bravery.

Qi jumped back to her feet. "Otto, Remy, get Mrs Ruane back to the *Beauty*, and the ship ready to lift."

"Oui, *Capitaine*."

Without waiting to see them comply Qi ran towards the bushes just as Ichiro disappeared into them. There was another gunshot. Qi pushed through the branches and almost tripped over the prone body of the man she had shot, which surprised her as much as it had probably surprised him.

Her cheek blazed with pain as another shot went off. She saw Ichiro pick up a third man and pull him into a bear hug. She didn't wait to see the result but ran past them and leapt the small smoky fire with a pan of vegetables nestled in the embers.

She emerged from the copse just in time to see two horses kicking into a fast canter. Kehal urged on his horse and held tight to the reins of the other on which Dhavni was perched, clinging to the saddle.

Qi hesitated. She was not a good rider and, if she gave chase, she would be alone. She could not fire on them because she might hit the woman. She sighed, and released the energy and tension that had built up in her. No.

Quickly she headed back into the trees. Ichiro had dropped his opponent, who was now lying on the ground moaning. Qi smiled at Ichiro and patted him on the arm. She pointed at the man and gestured for Ichiro to pick him up and take him to the ship. Ichiro bent down, lifted him as if he weighed nothing and flung him across his shoulder.

Qi went back out and untied two of the horses. She mounted one and headed along the lake shore towards the ridge. She saw Terry stand and wave, whereupon she cantered across to him and he mounted the spare.

Together they headed back to the ship, collecting the last horse on the way. They would be able to sell the beasts, if nothing else.

* * *

They got the horses tied up and tightly hobbled on board to ensure they could not react badly when reduced gravity was engaged. Remy had Otto and Fanning on stoking. The steam pressure was up and the envelopes hot, so only the full weight of the *Beauty* held it on the ground.

Qi ignored the questioning looks of Fanning and Mrs Cameron. She strode up to the bridge, gave a couple of blasts on the klaxon, paused for a moment, then engaged the Faraday.

The *Frozen Beauty* leapt into the air.

17

Kehar Chabak suppressed the desire to flee as fast as possible. He could not risk the horses on such uneven and rocky terrain. He kept his body flat along his horse's neck and maintained a firm grasp of the reins of the other.

With luck they would not shoot for fear of hitting his rebellious sister. What had gone wrong? All his men dead or captured. He shook himself. It didn't matter because he had enough money to buy an army. And he still had his sister to marry off to Opinder Jandoo, though time was short.

There were no more shots fired. The path bent round a prominence made from an ancient avalanche of rocks. Within moments they were out of sight. The track followed the cliffs to the left and dropped away into the river valley on the right.

He kept the horses at a canter but relaxed the pace a little. But he could not afford to be lazy; Jandoo was waiting for his bride.

"I hate you, Kehar."

"Shut up or I will beat you."

"You will not escape the British."

"That is no concern." He turned in the saddle and looked at his pathetic excuse for a sister. She was dirty but was otherwise pleasant enough to look at. Jandoo would be pleased with her, and especially with the dowry Kehar offered.

Kehar turned back to watch the trail. He grinned to himself. Jandoo had agreed to take his sister as bride for just fifty of the British sterling. Only a tenth of Kehar's new wealth.

Connection through marriage to Jandoo would give Kehar the respect he deserved, and the remaining money would make him a place in the world. It had been a gift from the gods when Dhavni had come crying to him about her disagreement with the other woman.

At first she had gone along with his plan to blackmail the woman into giving him some money because she wanted to teach the shameful Westerner a lesson.

Now he had seen the female viper with his own eyes. Tall and ugly, even if she did have pale skin. And the colour of her hair was like the mud that bubbled up at the hot springs. He almost shuddered as he recalled her.

The weather was dry and overcast and the wind a little chill but they were making good progress. He did not want to tire the horses, so he let them relax back into a trot and looped the reins of the other horse over his saddle's pommel so he did not have to hold on.

They descended into the next valley where the terrain became greener. The trees managed to retain their leaves, and the wind was less cold. The sound of the tumbling river grew in their ears.

Kehar was not bored with the journey as it afforded him time to imagine what he would do with the money. A cold knife sliced through his heart as he realised he had not taken the opportunity to check that it was all there. He stopped and dismounted. His hands almost shook as he took down the bag and fiddled with the metal buckles.

"Having difficulty, little brother?" she said. "Want your big sister to open that bag for you? What are you going to do if they cheated you the way you cheated them?"

He glared at her. "The first thing I will do if they have cheated me is to kill you." He was satisfied with the look of fear that flashed across her face. She sat back in the saddle and was silent.

He got the bag open and rifled through the large printed sheets. He couldn't read, but there were many, many sheets and the British king frowned at him from every one.

"You see?" said Dhavni. "She cares for me, and she wants me back."

"Do not speak of shameful things. Or I will shut your mouth for you."

* * *

The *Frozen Beauty* hung at a height of five thousand feet above the valley floor. Qi stood on the upper deck. The cold wind cut through her outer coat and leather jerkin, finding its way inside to bare skin and freezing it.

She did not care. The heat of her anger was proof against the cold. That rat of a brother had never intended to give up his sister. Of course Kathleen had been a fool to even consider paying such an enormous sum to such a criminal.

Dingbang had tried to persuade her to leave but Qi was personally offended by this Kehar Chabak. She was going to take him back to Captain Reynolds as a peace offering—it might assuage his hurt at being left behind and prevent him from issuing a warrant for her and her crew's arrest.

She looked down through the binoculars. The two were on the move again; they had stopped for something, though she had not been able to see what it was. The *Beauty* was in no danger of losing them since Kehar was simply following the trail that led along the valley.

"I brought you a drink, Captain," said Fanning.

Qi let the binoculars hang loose on their strap around her neck and took the steaming tin mug. She smelled coffee, and felt it revive her as it slipped down her throat.

The *Beauty* surged slightly as Dingbang engaged the thrusters to push them ahead against the wind.

"Is that a village up ahead?" said Fanning. A slight haze of smoke hung over a patch of ground in the distance.

"More than a village," said Qi, studying it through the binoculars. "A small town."

18

Kehar and Dhavni trotted over the last ridge and headed down into the town. Many of the buildings were stone, and there was a mosque with a minaret. It had a market most days. But this had one feature that set it apart from other towns of a similar size. There were no British.

Perhaps the fact the place could not easily be reached from the coast side of the mountains, and one had to seek it out if coming from the other side, had caused it to be missed. Whatever the reason, it was a sample of what life could be like without the British controlling every action.

Kehar headed for a money-changer he knew on the banking street and converted one of the notes into something he could use. He did not trust anyone enough to leave the money anywhere. He would carry it where he could feel it next to his skin.

Next he spent some of it on better quality clothes for both himself and Dhavni. Not too ostentatious since he did not want to attract attention. He hired a couple of men to carry their baggage, and a girl not only to attend his sister but also to keep an eye on her.

He made it clear to the girl that Dhavni was a reluctant bride and that if she disappeared the girl would pay with her life. Just to be sure, he hobbled Dhavni as if she were a horse.

Kehar smiled to himself. The ability to take what he wanted invigorated him. He even felt magnanimous towards his sister and allowed her some time to clean herself up—under the watchful eye of the maid.

Jandoo's astrologer had declared that the best time for their wedding was at sunset. That suited Jandoo, who never rose before

the midday meal, and it had meant Kehar was able to get Dhavni
ready in time.

* * *

The town was in shadow as the evening drew in. The sun had passed
down behind the mountains. Kehar rubbed his hands together, trying
to wipe the sweat from them.

"The hands of a liar are never dry," said Dhavni.

"Perhaps Jandoo will cut your tongue from your mouth."

"I will not wed Jandoo."

"You have no choice, sister," he said. "As our parents are no
longer here it is my responsibility to see you are disposed of
appropriately. And I can think of nothing more fitting."

"The gods will strike you down for the evil you do."

"The gods do not care."

On the other side of the room the two guards were playing
cards. The maid sat by Dhavni.

The call to prayer echoed across the town.

"Let us go."

Dhavni climbed to her feet without enthusiasm. The maid
prodded her to make her go faster.

"Gag her," said Kehar.

"Don't you dare!"

Kehar pulled out his gun.

"You would not dare harm me. What value would I be then?"

Kehar pointed the gun at the maid who squealed in terror. "You
always had a soft heart, Dhavni. If you do not accept a gag I will
shoot her." Then he added as an afterthought, "I can always buy
another maid. How many would we need to go through?"

Dhavni allowed the girl to tie a strip of cloth around her mouth.

"You see?" said Kehar. "Why must you argue every time? You never win."

* * *

The *Beauty* had settled in a small valley a mile from the town. And, after careful consideration of the options, Qi set off with Fanning, Otto and Mrs Ruane, leaving the rest on board. She had not wanted to take Kathleen but the woman had insisted.

Qi had hoped they might be relatively inconspicuous, but Mrs Ruane proved incapable of it.

They had reached the outskirts of the town and waited in a stable while Fanning, with the judicious application of money to specific palms, had determined that one Opinder Jandoo was to wed Dhavni Chabak, who was reputed to have a handsome dowry, this very evening.

"I'll tear his heart from his chest," growled Mrs Ruane. "Using my money to sell his sister. She'd sooner kill herself than let a man touch her."

"She wouldn't be the first," said Fanning. "Seems his wives often die by their own hand. Except when they die by his."

Qi frowned at Fanning. Providing more fuel for Mrs Ruane's anger was unhelpful. She changed the subject. "Did you find out anything about this Opinder Jandoo?"

"Local bigwig hoodlum," said Fanning. Their confused faces prompted further explanation. "Criminal boss. Owns the town. Likes to make out he's sophisticated or something."

"So how do we get into this wedding?"

"Oh, easy, it's always a public show. Likes to keep his people happy."

"The only problem," said Qi. "Is that the brother knows what we look like."

"Oh, I got that covered," said Fanning. Qi did not like the grin on her face.

* * *

Mrs Ruane had not offered more than a token protest when Fanning told her to dye her hair and darken her face. They dressed her in a men's *salwar kameez* and, with a dagger in her belt, she looked reasonably male apart from her bust. She and Qi went into one of the animal stalls and suppressed her proportions with some turns of cloth. She would not pass a detailed examination, but that shouldn't be required.

With a change of clothes Fanning passed for a servant, which meant no one would look at her, while Otto was outfitted in a slightly ill-fitting *salwar kameez* and had his skin darkened as well. He kept pulling at the cloth trying to get comfortable.

"Would it not have been better to choose *Herr* Montgomery or Darras, captain? This Kehal has seen me."

Qi considered telling the truth—he was the most expendable—but that would have been cruel. "On balance you were the best choice. Ichiro cannot hear, Darras cannot shoot well and Montgomery cannot fight."

Mrs Ruane helped Qi into a sari. It felt very odd; she could not remember the last time she had worn women's clothing. Still her skin tone was good and as long as she kept her face down people probably would not notice her Chinese features. She managed to conceal a knife and gun under the extensive folds.

She sent Fanning out to acquire a cart and driver.

And within half an hour they arrived outside the opulent and extensive home of Opinder Jandoo where perhaps a hundred people waiting to enter.

19

There were armed guards at the door but their examination of those entering was cursory at best. It was difficult to maintain close attention for long periods of time. They seemed mostly concerned with keeping out the beggars, who were directed around to the side where they were being fed.

Qi and her party got through the gates and followed the crowd into the central courtyard. There were more guards, their guns conspicuous at their sides, located at the entrance. Once she was inside, Qi saw still more guards up on the balcony.

Opinder Jandoo must do very well for himself, thought Qi as she looked around. The courtyard was flagged in a black stone she did not recognise. Plants and trees in pots had been situated to break up the open space and allow for groups to form.

There were no obvious routes up to the balcony, which was stone with painted wooden railings. A few clouds dotted the blue of the sky.

A waiter came around with a tray of fruit drinks. Qi took the one that looked like orange juice. She tasted it and felt the tang of lime following the initial hit of orange. She checked her gun and knife.

The air was filled with the sound of people laughing and talking while musicians played in the background. This did not seem like a normal wedding as far as she understood Indian weddings. The ceremony took hours and nothing appeared to be happening.

"Where is Dhavni?" Mrs Ruane was trying to keep the pitch of her voice low to make it sound male. Qi did not think it was very effective, but in the general hubbub no one noticed. Qi looked around. She would have thought that Mrs Ruane would be able to see more clearly since she was taller, but perhaps she was distracted.

"They should be in the main building," said Qi. "They won't have the wedding out here."

The disguised party moved through the throng, squeezing between groups in deep discussion, others laughing uproariously, and the occasional doe-eyed youngsters eyeing each other across an empty space.

On the far side of the courtyard from the main entrance was a pair of double-doors with a pair of more efficient-looking guards. They had guns and swords, and beneath their turbans their eyes watched everyone who came near.

Qi turned her back on them and the others drew round her. Qi pulled out her watch and glanced at the time. It would be sundown very soon. Looking up she saw the sky darkening; the sun had left the mountain tops in the east. She noticed several servants lighting lamps around the courtyard, and whispered in Fanning's ear. With a smile Fanning headed off.

"Head towards the bigger guard," Qi said to Mrs Ruane. "I'll follow behind like a dutiful wife. When you get close I'll do the rest."

"What is it I should do?" asked Otto in a low voice.

"Walk beside Mrs Ruane. Be ready to go inside."

A man walked past and looked at Qi. She remembered just before it became awkward that she shouldn't look him in the face.

"When will I know the correct time?"

"You'll know," snapped Qi. She saw Fanning intercepting one of the lamplighters.

"Go, Kathleen. Now."

Mrs Ruane's long strides carried her towards the guard so quickly that both Otto and Qi had to half-run to keep up with her. Even so, Qi was careful to remain a few steps behind.

There was a shout from behind them, a shout of anger turned to fear. And every person in the courtyard seemed to hold their breath and look. The guard, too, was looking past them.

Then there were more shouts, warnings of danger. Mrs Ruane came to a stop beside the guard, who did not notice as Qi closed in on him, rummaging beneath her clothing for the knife.

"*Namaste*," she said. He looked down at her in confusion. She placed the steel of the blade between his legs. "Do you speak English? Just nod if you do."

He opened his mouth to speak and she jammed the knife a little harder into his groin. This seemed to activate his memory and he just nodded. Qi relieved him of his gun and sword, dropping them to the floor behind a potted plant.

"Very good. We are not here to hurt anyone, just to collect something that belongs to us. Do you understand?"

He nodded. His attention was fixed on Qi and the blade.

Otto had pulled out his gun and moved to the door.

"You will escort us inside. My friends have guns, as do I. If you raise the alarm I will shoot you."

He nodded. The noise from the people in the courtyard was increasing in volume: shouts of terror, screams, running sandals slapping on the stones.

"Very good," she said. "You go first."

With everything under control Qi glanced round. A blaze engulfed the eastern wall, consuming the stalls, tables and food that had been laid out. The light fabrics across the windows on the ground and upper floors were erupting into flame and floating off, setting fire to anything flammable they touched.

Fanning came trotting up.

"I said a *small* fire," said Qi.

"You can't have too much of a good thing," said Fanning. "Besides, I didn't expect the place to go up like Fourth of July rockets." She wandered up to the door where Otto had his gun trained on the guard. "Shall we enter, Captain?"

At that moment the door was thrown back from the inside and a crowd of people fled the building. The guard went for Otto's gun by grabbing at his arm. Qi kicked the back of his knee, forcing him down and off-balance, then threw her weight against his shoulder and slammed his head into the wall.

He slumped to the ground.

"Come on," she said as the others stared at her.

The initial rush of wedding guests had petered out and they pushed past the stragglers into a large well-appointed room. The floor was of herringbone wood up from which jutted carved wooden pillars. The walls were brightly painted with depictions of—Qi blushed and put her attention on the group that remained.

She recognised Kehal and Dhavni, and she assumed the large older man to be Opinder Jandoo. He was arguing with another man who was standing behind a large table with a thick sheaf of papers.

There were three guards, each armed with a gun and a sword.

"Kathleen!" Dhavni's voice echoed round the room and Jandoo's remonstrations ceased as he saw the newcomers.

Qi stepped forward and pulled the sari back from her head. She held the sword loosely in her left hand and the gun in her right.

"Who are you?" said Jandoo in good English.

"I have no argument with you, Opinder Jandoo," said Qi. "I am Captain Qi Zang. I come only to take back those things that are not Kehal Chabak's to give."

The guards moved in a few steps.

"And what are those things, woman?" He sounded amused, which gave Qi the sinking feeling that they might have to fight.

"Dhavni Chabak and the money Kehal acquired by deceit."

Behind him the man finished gathering up the papers and backed away from the group.

Jandoo shrugged. "The girl is betrothed to me, the money is my dowry."

"Not all of it," said Kehal like a child. Jandoo looked at him and made a movement with his hand. A single shot shattered the air. Kehal looked surprised. He wavered for a moment and then sank to his knees. He would have fallen to the floor but his sister knelt beside him, holding him by the shoulders.

Qi glanced at her associates. Otto might have gone pale beneath the blacking, and his hand was at his mouth. Mrs Ruane had not moved and the gun was firm in her hand. Fanning was—nowhere to be seen.

Kehal slipped to the floor, dragging Dhavni down with him.

"He is no loss," said Jandoo. "And now I shall have all the money as dowry."

The smell of smoke drifted in. Jandoo frowned and looked past the intruders. "What have you done?"

"The money, Jandoo, or we will all burn," said Qi.

The man laughed and grabbed Dhavni by her upper arm, yanking her to her feet. "There are other ways out, woman." He glanced around and picked out the man with the book. "Bring the *Sri Guru Granth Sahib*, we will do this outside."

"You have the money, just leave the girl," shouted Mrs Ruane taking several steps forward.

Jandoo paused. "So that's what this is about? Another suitor?" Then he stopped and beneath the fading light through the sky lights he peered at her.

"Another woman?" He roared with laughter. Dhavni squirmed in his grip, grabbed the ceremonial knife from his waistband and pushed it hard into his stomach.

"Up here!" Fanning's voice echoed through the room over the increasing snapping and roaring of burning wood. Qi looked up and saw Fanning on a balcony. The guard they had caught looked at her. She nodded. "Get out of here, and take your friends."

He took off fast for a big man, towards a door in the back. Jandoo reached out to him with hands anointed in his own blood, and said something Qi could not make out. The guard spat at him and ran on.

Jandoo fell to his knees, the front of his ceremonial clothes soaked with glistening red.

The heat from the flames now licking the inside of the hall pressed against Qi's back.

"Come on!" shouted Fanning. "The stairs." She pointed to the side of the hall where steps led upwards. Qi looked back and saw Mrs Ruane with Dhavni, hugging her.

"Captain, look," said Otto. He was pointing up. She followed his line and saw a shadow drifting across the skylight. *Beauty*.

"Go help Fanning and the ship. We'll be following."

As Otto ran off, Qi strode over to the embracing couple. They were oblivious to her. She glanced down at Jandoo. He wasn't dead yet but was deflating like a punctured balloon.

She turned back to Kathleen and Dhavni, and cleared her throat. "You can do that on the ship. Time to go." She picked up the bag with the money and headed for the stairs.

20

"I should arrest you, Captain Zang."

"To what end, Captain Reynolds?"

"My personal satisfaction in repairing my damaged pride."

"I would have thought being instrumental in taking down a major criminal would satisfy that desire quite thoroughly."

Reynolds sighed. "It does."

The *Frozen Beauty* had squeezed onto the back lawn of the Ruane estate on the morning of the following day, crushing the croquet hoops. They had been instantly surrounded by Captain Reynolds and his troops, who had returned as soon as the deception had been revealed and his scouts had found the dead bandits.

Captain Reynolds watched as Mrs Ruane and her paramour disappeared into the building. He shook his head. None of the other crew had disembarked but Qi had related the sequence of events.

He thrust out his hand which Qi shook. "I hope you have clear skies, Captain Zang."

Qi gave him a bow of respect then turned and climbed the ladder to the top deck. She gave him a short wave and disappeared from sight.

Captain Reynolds took a few steps back as the klaxon in the ship sounded three times. Butterfly wings stroked across his skin as the Faraday engaged.

The *Frozen Beauty* seemed to take a breath, then fell into the sky.

BOOK 3

DR MORBURY'S CARGO

1

Fanning backed towards the door of the bridge, the one that led to the cargo hold. She was out of sight of Otto now and could no longer see the navigator's face twisted in anger.

"Check your course, von Krone!"

Otto said something in German. Angry. Arguing with Captain Qi, who spun round and pointed a gun at him. "Check the course, we have to reach our destination on time. We must stay on course. We must be on time."

The deck of the Frozen Beauty vibrated beneath Fanning's feet. The captain was driving the ship hard. They must be burning coal as if it were as cheap as moonshine.

Otto shouted something in German again.

"English!" screamed Captain Qi. Then she shouted in Chinese. "English, you idiot."

"We are on course, Captain," he growled without the slightest respect in his voice. "Let me have Fanning, Captain!"

Fanning reached behind her and turned the handle of the door. Without a sound she pushed it open.

"You stay at your post, Herr von Krone," yelled the captain. "Check the course!"

"I just told you!"

"Check the course, von Krone," she said, then more Chinese. "Or I'll blow your brains out."

As silent as the grave, Fanning slipped through the open door and closed it without the slightest click. There was neither key nor bolt, which was a shame. If she could have trapped the two of them on the bridge it would have made her feel a little more safe.

The short companionway was all greys and shadow. Light filtered around the edges of the trapdoor to the upper deck. Fanning leaned back against the door. The two people on the bridge continued to shout at one another: the captain demanding Otto check the course, he arguing, wanting to "have" Fanning, as if she were a possession, and then obeying.

Fanning felt in her pocket for her pipe and tobacco pouch. By touch she pushed a thick wad into the bowl and pressed it down with her thumb. She slipped the pouch back into the pocket and fished out her box of Vestas.

As they rattled one against the other, she cringed. She opened the box and removed a match, carefully closing it again afterwards, and struck the tip against the rough side of the box. It sparked but did not catch. She did it again.

The flare of the match half-blinded her. Then she saw Mrs Cameron's face across the companionway in the dark. The woman was staring at her. Fanning hesitated, then touched the flaring tip to the bowl and sucked hard. The flame disappeared into the bowl.

She could only see Beatrice's eyes reflecting the light. Eyes with pupils so wide they hid any colour in the iris, just like Otto's and the captain's. If the eyes were truly gateways to the soul, these gates had been ripped away completely.

The flame reared up again. In the bowl, the tobacco glowed red. Mrs Cameron's head was fully illuminated now: hair dishevelled, cheeks streaked where tears had fallen and then dried. Fanning sucked the match flame down into the bowl once more.

This time the tobacco glowed with a certainty that it would not now go out. Fanning pulled away the match, extinguishing it with a shake of her hand. She dropped it to the floor and ground out the remaining ember.

Drawing in a lungful of burning pipe-smoke, Fanning felt its calming and restorative power flow through her. She breathed it out, careful not to blow it directly at Mrs Cameron.

She brought her hand to her forehead in salute. "Ma'am."

"What are you, Fanning?" Beatrice asked, her voice was tremulous. Fanning's eyes adjusted to the greyness. Mrs Cameron was pressed back against the wall. She glanced here and there, as if she feared something would leap on her at any moment.

"Ma'am?" Fanning knew what Mrs Cameron was talking about, but no one had ever challenged her so directly on her duality. Fanning was so adjusted to it, she did not even notice.

"Are you a man or a woman, Fanning?"

"Can't rightly say, Mrs Cameron," she said. "Is that a thing you have a powerful yearning to know?"

"I don't know whether I should be afraid of you."

"No need to be afraid, ma'am, either way," said Fanning. "I won't hurt you none."

"That's what they all say," she hissed and threw herself at Fanning.

To say that Fanning expected the attack would be an exaggeration, but given recent events it was not wholly unexpected, either. She moved easily to avoid the knife Mrs Cameron held high and inefficiently. It slammed into the wall where Fanning's head had been just a moment before.

Fanning felt very guilty as she punched the woman in the side. She had said she would not hurt her, but Beatrice had made Fanning into a liar. Her hand hit something ribbed and hard. Mrs Cameron turned on her, seemingly unaffected.

Being a traditional British lady, Beatrice Cameron was fond of her boned undergarments which, on this occasion, acted as armour. Fanning dodged as Beatrice swung a wild blow at her head. The knife remained embedded in the wall.

"I won't let you hurt me!" she said as she threw another untrained punch at Fanning's face.

It really was quite awkward. There was no chance Mrs Cameron would hurt her except through dumb luck, but Fanning was keen not to damage Beatrice if at all possible. Like most, if not all, of the crew, Beatrice was overwrought and not in her right mind. She would no doubt regret her actions when she regained her senses.

Fanning dodged past her and headed along the companionway. She turned her back on her assailant—perhaps not the wisest move, but it was quicker that way.

She reached the door to the cabin Mrs Cameron shared with the captain. Fanning had agreed that, for the sake of Mrs Cameron's honour, it would be better if she bunked with the captain, who was more obviously a woman than Fanning was.

Fanning had grabbed and turned the handle of the door when something heavy hit her between the shoulders. Her forehead slammed into the door. Stupid. Should not have turned her back.

The door fell open and she stumbled inside on unsteady legs. There was a scream behind her and Mrs Cameron hit her again, this time in the middle of her back. Fanning went down, and the deck did not treat her head any more favourably than the door had.

Something heavy and wearing skirts landed on Fanning's spine. If the ship had not been running under the Faraday, Fanning imagined Mrs Cameron would have knocked the wind out of her. As it was she had Fanning pinned, but it would only take a moment to throw her off since her weight was considerably less than it would normally be.

Mrs Cameron did not give her the chance.

Fanning's head was yanked up and back by her hair. Then her face was repeatedly slammed into the solid wood of the deck. She could hear the noise of each impact reverberating, partly through the room and partly around the inside of her head.

She clung to consciousness, embarrassed that she had been bested by the least combative member of the crew. With every battering blow, her grip on the real world grew weaker until it was gone completely.

2

Yesterday Afternoon

Qi frowned as one of the dockworkers tripped and fell against the door support. The box he was carrying slipped from his fingers and he bent at the knees in a vain attempt to catch it before it hit the ground. He only succeeded in getting his hand caught under it. A solid thump echoed through the cargo bay.

A stream of invective poured from his mouth and he sucked on his bruised fingers. The small crate toppled over and made another less noisy crash. Qi hoped there was nothing important inside.

"Are you listening, Captain?"

Qi turned her attention back to Mrs Cameron. "I'm sorry, Beatrice, what were you saying?"

Beatrice Cameron was decked out in her best European garb complete, from the look of her thin waist, with tightly bound corset. She wondered who had pulled it tight for her. Mrs Cameron might sleep in her cabin but Qi was only there for a few hours a night. Fanning?

"I realise I asked to be brought to the Fortress, and that was all." She stopped and glanced across the air-dock. Qi followed her gaze. Beyond the cargo area where the Frozen Beauty was docked were the buildings of the passenger embarkation lounge; then came some of the military buildings and standing over it all, Sigiriya.

Sigiriya. The great upthrust of granite located near the middle of Ceylon, where the British had chosen to build their enormous naval dockyard. And almost directly above, seven thousand miles into the Void, hung the Queen Victoria Station: the route to every other world.

"But?" said Qi.

A steam-driven Faraday truck puffed up to the ship, loaded down with more crates belonging to Dr Morbury. Eight workers gathered round to unload it.

"I—I would like to stay on board."

Qi's attention snapped around. She had been willing to share her cabin for the duration of this trip because she felt she owed Mrs Cameron a debt for helping her keep the Frozen Beauty from the clutches of the Chinese thugs who claimed to own it.

They did own it, in all truth, but that did not mean Qi was going to let them have it. So she had been grateful enough to provide Beatrice Cameron with free passage to Ceylon to escape her husband.

"What capacity would you see yourself filling on board my ship, Beatrice?" said Qi.

"Cook?"

"Mr Montgomery is a perfectly good cook, I don't need another one."

Beatrice hesitated. "But it would free him up; he is your engineer."

"The two are not mutually exclusive."

"Chaperone for Fanning."

Qi laughed. "Even Fanning does not have an adequate job description; he's just a cabin boy."

"Someone should look after her—him."

Qi glanced up. Fanning was leaning over the rail on the top deck, smoking his pipe. "I do not think Fanning needs a nursemaid."

Mrs Cameron frowned. "There must be something I can do."

There were shouts from the dock workers as they manhandled the heavy apparatus from the truck down onto the deck and pushed it on runners inside. The trundling sound echoed through the ship.

"It is not that I do not like you, Beatrice," said Qi. "But I am running a business and I do not give free rides."

"I'll pay."

"Why? You can go back to England, or anywhere else, from here. Or even the Americas, where no one knows who you are and would care even less."

"What would I do in the Americas, Captain?" said Mrs Cameron, her voice desolate. "Walk the streets because, as you have so ably pointed out, I have no useful skills."

"I am sorry."

"I have offered to pay."

"And I refuse to take your money," said Qi. "You will squander it on travelling with us and then you will truly be destitute. I will not have that on my conscience."

The second machine was being offloaded. The men were competent enough, but if she had been in charge of the process she would have slowed them down. They were damaging the cargo.

Still, that was not her concern in this instance. The Beauty was solely for transportation; getting the cargo to its destination was her only responsibility.

Calcutta was close to the Chinese border and under the sway of the gangs, two things which composed a potential concern. But selling the cargo was not required; all they had to do was open the doors and let it be offloaded. They had already been paid for this journey, and for the return trip carrying one of the botanists plus the travel agent.

Mrs Cameron pulled out her kerchief and dabbed at her cheek. A diesel-powered carriage rumbled up to the Beauty and three men extricated themselves from it. The two younger ones, perhaps in their thirties, treated the third, who was old enough to have white hair, with considerable deference.

Qi neither liked nor understood these people. When Dingbang had returned to the ship explaining that he had the commission she was pleased, since carrying passengers and cargo was simpler than cutting ice. Then she had met them, which put a whole new face on the situation. Dr Morbury was a very rude man, and the less she had to do with him the better.

She glanced back at Beatrice. "You can stay on board for this trip."

"How much?"

"I will not charge you for the reason I gave and I will not set a precedent," said Qi. "You can, however, liaise with our passengers. I find them difficult to talk to."

Mrs Cameron suppressed the excitement that reddened her cheeks. "Thank you so much," she said. "I will do such a good job you will want to keep me."

"I doubt it, Beatrice," said Qi. "As I have made quite plain, we do not carry passengers as a rule."

"When shall I start?"

Qi nodded in the direction of the three men heading in their direction. "Immediately. Make sure everything is to their satisfaction and deal with their accommodation."

*   *   *

To Beatrice's eye, the captain turned and faded from view into the dark interior of the ship. She smoothed down the front of her dress, made one final dab at her eyes to dry them, and then turned towards the oncoming group.

She smiled pleasantly. "Gentlemen, welcome to the Frozen Beauty. My name is Mrs Beatrice Cameron and I will be your ship's liaison for the journey." She held out her hand to the older gentleman, who squinted at her. A monocle dangled from his lapel.

He took her hand in a weak grasp and gave it a gentle shake. "A woman?"

Mrs Cameron's smile did not falter. "My dear sir, your captain is also a woman."

"Damn suffragists."

The smile remained in place but any genuine good humour had drained out of her. The captain had certainly given her the worst possible job, presumably as her punishment for nagging.

"And you are, sir?" she said keeping her voice calm. *May I have the pleasure of knowing who is insulting me?*

After a moment's hesitation the youngest of the three stepped forwards. "This is Dr Morbury, the Curator of the Botanic Garden in Oxford."

He said the name of the garden with such significance Beatrice could only assume it was important. Though she looked expectantly in his direction, the great man did not nod his head or acknowledge her in any way.

"And Dr Lambington."

"Mrs Cameron," said the second man. He smiled pleasantly but did not offer his hand. He was only in his thirties but already losing his hair, and was quite rotund.

"And I am Tom Ketteridge," he said and held out his hand.

She shook it. "A pleasure, Dr Ketteridge."

The old man spluttered.

"Just Mr Ketteridge. I am responsible for the various travel arrangements."

"My apologies, Mr Ketteridge," she said. "I am delighted to welcome you all on board."

“I hope we will have the opportunity to be introduced to all of the crew?”

“Speak for yourself, man,” said Dr Morbury.

“I’m sure that can be arranged, Mr Ketteridge,” said Beatrice, surprised at her own strength of will in suppressing her desire to strike out at the rudeness of the curator.

3

Now

Fanning came awake with the awareness that her throat and tongue were very dry. And that her forehead was throbbing.

She blinked her eyes open. She was no longer face down on the floor but face up on a bed. The ceiling was a fuzzy grey, illuminated by the dim light from the porthole.

The reason for the dryness in her mouth came to her; she was completely unable to breathe through her nose. She made to reach up with her left hand to touch it but found her arm would not move. Her wrist was tied. Both were tied. She squinted along her nose; it looked larger than usual, and in the dim light she could see patches of congealed blood.

The beating she had received at the hands of Mrs Cameron had not been a dream at all. She wondered how long she had been unconscious. Long enough for it to have become dusk, apparently. It was difficult to understand what had happened. Even more difficult to understand why she was unaffected.

Assuming she was unaffected. The possibility that everyone else was entirely sane and she was the one that had gone mad crossed her mind. She rejected it, as both of her minds were aware of the other and each of them knew the other had not changed.

It had been difficult when her brother Frank had joined her inside her head. She preferred to think of it that way rather than the truth of it, that her brother had been forced in. It was not a pleasant memory and it had taken a lot of work to just let him be, and even let him take charge. There were times when she was no longer sure whether it was the original her or her brother that was in control.

He had always been bossy because he was older. When their parents died Frank had looked out for her, and he did not see why that arrangement should change just because he was now sharing her body.

Truth was he had been scared to start with—not that he liked to admit it—and she had been the one that had looked after him. But once he had gotten used to the way things were he just did what he always had. Told her what to do.

But that weren't getting them nowhere.

They were the only ones still in command of their senses. The others seemed to have entirely lost theirs.

She felt the cords that bound her. Stockings, if she was not mistaken. She tried lifting her head. It throbbed mightily as she did so but she saw she was still in the captain's cabin. This was Mrs Cameron's bed. And she was here too, sitting on the floor with her back to the door, but asleep. When the ship was light sleeping became a lot easier, even in the oddest of positions.

Fanning's throbbing head forced her to settle back. It must be the cargo doing this. That was the only explanation. She knew the passengers were plant collectors but she had not taken any interest in them or their cargo. Scientists made her uncomfortable.

As the only one still in charge of their reason it was up to her to save the day, which she would do but for the fact she had been beaten by the weakest member of the crew and was now restrained.

She tested the ties. There was a lot of play but the knots seemed firm. Somehow she had to get out. There was probably no way of doing that without waking Mrs Cameron, so she needed to get untied fast.

By sliding her body over, Fanning found she could get her hand into her pocket. She pulled out the box of matches. Silk was strong but burnt easily. Fanning twisted her hand and found that she could get her fingers under the cord so if she had a lighted match in her fingers she should be able to burn through it.

She jumped as Mrs Cameron snuffled and snored for a moment, muttering words. Fanning could not make them out exactly but they held the tone of someone pleading for mercy. The woman even cried out and moaned as if in pain.

Fanning managed to slide the small tray out of the box of matches. Fumbling, she dumped the contents onto the bed. She sighed and set about putting them into her pocket. She did not want them catching light and burning her to death.

Fairly sure she'd got them all, Fanning wedged the matchbox under her rear end to hold it firm. She retrieved one of the matches and dragged it along the strip on the side of the box.

She winced at the noise but Mrs Cameron did not stir at the sound.

The match did not light. Fanning tried again, striking harder and faster. She missed the box completely and cussed her own ineptitude. Third time's a charm, she thought.

It wasn't. Nor the fourth.

Finally the familiar hiss, and the burst of chemical incandescence lit the room. Awkwardly Fanning twisted her fingers and felt the heat on her wrist. She twisted her whole body to make it easier to get the match under the cord without burning her own precious skin.

I'll have to buy Beatrice some new stockings, she thought as her hand came free. The heat from the match burnt her fingers and she dropped it. The light vanished.

She sat up and made sure the match had gone out. Her head pounded at the sudden movement and she wished she hadn't. Mrs Cameron did not stir. Fanning managed to undo the other knotted stocking and then did the same for her ankles. She kept glancing over to Mrs Cameron against the possibility she might wake.

Then she was free, and jumped to the deck light as a feather.

Looking down at the sleeping form of Mrs Cameron, she weighed up her choices. Leaving by the door was best, which meant Mrs Cameron would awake. Frank would not hit a woman. Liza herself had no problem with it, but Frank made the rules.

She untied the stocking from the bed and stretched it out. Kneeling by Mrs Cameron's feet she looped the stocking twice round her ankles, loosely, and made a slipknot. She was surprised how tight she had it before Mrs Cameron came awake.

Fanning yanked the slipknot tight as Mrs Cameron kicked out in reaction. She grabbed Beatrice's left wrist before the woman had come fully to her senses. With her foot on Mrs Cameron's ankle, Fanning yanked her arm hard. In a manoeuvre that would have been impossible in normal gravity, Fanning levered Mrs Cameron up and then over so she was face down on the floor.

Fanning nailed Beatrice to the floor with a knee in the middle of her backbone and wrenched her arm back. Beatrice squealed in pain. With her other hand Fanning grabbed the ankle-tie and pulled the woman's feet up to her wrist. She looped the tie around the wrist and drew it tight. Then she reached over and grabbed the other flailing arm and did the same.

Mrs Cameron was hog-tied.

"I don't know if it crossed your mind, but I wouldn't shout none, Beatrice," she said in the woman's ear. "Everyone's gone a little crazy and you wouldn't want them to find you like this, would you?"

Mrs Cameron said nothing. Fanning rummaged through her skirt until she found Beatrice's kerchief. She also fetched the other burnt stocking, then forced the cloth into the woman's mouth and tied it in place.

"You just rest there awhile and keep yourself quiet." Fanning lifted her easily and placed her on the bed. "I'll be back."

And if I'm not, she thought, it'll be because we're all knocking on heaven's door together.

4

Yesterday Afternoon

Mrs Cameron led the way into the cargo bay, the three men following.

"We do not have passenger quarters for everyone, this being a cargo vessel," she said and headed towards the front part of the cargo bay under the bridge. "However, we are preparing temporary accommodation."

Ichiro was holding a wooden frame while Terry pinned a cloth across it. Several similar frames had been stacked against the wall behind them. Vertical struts to hold the frames, thereby creating makeshift walls, were already in place.

"I realise it may not be what you are used to, Doctor Morbury," Beatrice continued. "However, it is only for a couple of days."

The professor harrumphed. "It might seem that way to you, Mrs Cameron," he said. "We have trekked the wilderness of Venus to bring our specimens home. This represents luxury compared to those conditions."

Beatrice smiled. "How nice," she said. "Then you'll be right at home."

"As long as they are ready on time."

Beatrice glanced at Terry, who nodded. "They will, of course, be quite ready.

"Would you like to inspect your cargo?" she asked out of courtesy, although she would have preferred to leave them. She had to remind herself she was trying to make a good impression so that the captain kept her aboard.

She knew she could maintain the illusion. Her husband had always been trying to make a good impression with his seniors by entertaining at home, requiring her to be the perfect hostess, a role at which she had succeeded. She had even continued to smile after Ellis Greatrix, one of the senior partners, had touched her inappropriately. He had always accepted her husband's invitations. She even had the idea that her husband had wanted her to "accommodate" the man, just so he would be promoted. She had not done so.

"I understand you are transferring plant samples?" said Beatrice conversationally as they walked across the cargo bay. On this side, Remy was at work with Otto installing pipes through from the engine room.

The Frenchman usually wore his work clothes since he was to be found on the upper deck tending the balloons. This was the first time, however, Beatrice had seen the young German computationer wearing anything other than a suit. In fact she was certain he did not own anything else. She concluded the overalls he wore must belong to Remy, as they were of the same design and were rolled up at the ankles. Remy was quite tall.

In response to her question the two younger scientists seemed to tighten up. The older man replied, "Yes. Living samples."

"Is it as hot on Venus as they say?"

"Yes, Mrs Cameron, the planet is considerably closer to the sun and is thus much hotter."

Remy grunted and muttered something in French under his breath. Mrs Cameron only caught part of it; it was not complimentary. She glanced nervously at the scientists, but if any of them had noticed they did not react.

Mrs Cameron turned away from the Frenchman. "So the plants need heat to survive?"

"That is correct," said Dr Lambington. "Once your fellow has prepared the heating elements we must switch it on."

"And you're going to Calcutta?"

At her words Dr Lambington exchanged glances with the Curator of the Botanic Garden and then returned his attention to Beatrice.

"If you don't mind me saying so," he said, "it seems unusual for a lady of your quality to be aboard a vessel such as this."

If he had intended to make her feel uncomfortable he had most certainly succeeded in his goal. She hesitated and found no convincing lie to tell.

"Allow me to show you the rest of the vessel so that you can get your bearings."

* * *

Qi went over the chart again. This was a simple cargo trip. In fact, it was entirely possible this could become a new type of business for them.

Carrying ice from the mountains to the cities was as reliable as any trade, which meant they were victim to all the usual problems with taxes, cargo loading and unloading, working in freezing temperatures, navigating treacherous mountains in a balloon craft. Not to mention the competition from the individual traders with two or three ships, and the big companies with dozens of vessels and their ability to buy coal, and other necessities, in bulk at lower prices.

And buy more than they needed to drive up the price for their rivals.

It had been a stroke of luck when Dingbang had fallen into conversation with Mr Ketteridge. The fellow was not a fool; he had recognised that a ship insulated against heat to prevent ice from melting in transit was equally insulated against the cold.

Or rather, protected in such a way that the plants they were transporting could be kept hot more easily than on another vessel without insulation.

The journey from the Fortress in Ceylon up to Calcutta would not take more than a couple of days and the scientists were willing to pay well for it. Perhaps this was a business opportunity, transporting exotic plants from the planets to locations across India. And why stop at India? They could travel across the world delivering items that others would have more difficulty in carrying.

And where would that get her?

The Beauty was her life; it was her soul. If she succeeded in running a business carrying such things, they would have to expand. They would need a faster ship in order to compete, because as soon as it was clear they had found a new trade others would come in, offering cheaper and faster transportation. The big transportation companies would muscle in and force her out of business.

She shook her head.

No. This was not a good plan. Just take these fellows where they wanted to go and let that be the end of it. Nothing in this world would make her give up her ship.

Which brought her once more to the question of Calcutta. It was in Bengal, less than half a day's journey from China. There were plenty of ice ships from the mountains that came down to that hell-hole.

They needed to be in and out as fast as possible.

She rubbed her right hand idly. It had been itching on and off for the last day; she tried not to scratch it because it just made things worse. He hadn't commented on it but Dingbang had also been scratching. Must be something in the air.

5

Now

Fanning opened the door a little way and peered out.

The companionway was dark. The sound of Qi still shouting at Otto filtered down through the gloom. Fanning was surprised, but glad, that the captain had not shot him. How many hours had this been going on? Fanning wondered what was wrong with them; the symptom seemed to be some sort of mania. The captain was obsessed with arriving on time and with Otto, but he had seemed inordinately interested in Fanning herself.

Mrs Cameron had an equally undefined concern eating at her. The upshot was that she wanted to tie Fanning up and did not trust her. That was not an unusual reaction but the intensity was inappropriate, especially from someone who already knew Fanning well.

That this behaviour stemmed from their cargo was not in question. Something about these plants from Venus caused folks to behave oddly. Fanning had seen how careless the dock workers had been bringing the equipment and the plants on board. Obviously there had been an escape.

She shut the door on the quietly complaining Mrs Cameron and crept towards the rear. The door to the "cold-lock" stood closed at the end of the passage.

Should she head directly inside? She did not know if the scientists were affected. They should be, as they were the closest to the plants.

Fanning hesitated. What would be the problem with entering the cargo hold from the cold-lock? It was too obvious and, if there was any danger at all, it would come from there.

What were the options?

Go up on to the top deck and then down at the rear of the ship. There was no door from the engine room to the cargo hold but the newly installed steam pipes went through the floor.

Final option: Climb out onto the side of the ship and go in through the access door. It should be locked, though that would not present more than a minute's delay. That seemed the most unexpected option.

Fanning decided, turning away from the cold-lock door. She returned to the ladder and climbed towards the top deck. After a quick look behind her, she slid back the bolt and pushed it up, making a gap of less than an inch. The sound of the wind rushing across the deck filled her ears.

She peered out and tried to take in as much as possible of the deck.

There was no sign of Remy.

She pushed the hatch up further and slipped out, keeping low to the deck, then let it down and bolted it on the outside. The wind from their forward movement flowed past her in a constant stream.

It crossed her mind that Remy might be untouched. Except for the fact he had spent a lot of time in the cargo hold when the plants were brought on board, making sure everything was working properly and at the right temperature.

Otto had assisted him and Otto was not his usual self, so it was best to assume the worst until she found matters to be otherwise. Avoiding Remy completely would be the best move.

Fanning crept towards the stern. Above her the envelope holding the seven giant balloons that kept the ship aloft rippled and flowed as the Beauty travelled through the air.

Remy was a genius with hot air balloons. Even Fanning, who was not technical, could appreciate the cleverness of the design. Rather than having fires heating the air inside the balloons—like all the other ice cargo vessels of this type—they ran steam from the engines through pipes into the balloons and heated the air that way.

She glanced out past the deck towards the horizon. Across the broad yellows and greens of India the sun was going down. They were several miles out from the coast. Fanning guessed that Qi was running them across a bay as a short cut. But if they lost the light, they would only be able to steer by their compass.

It was not that they were likely to bump into anything over the ocean at night; most air traffic except the really big ships spent the dark hours on the ground. But they were over water and, in Qi's current state of mind, it was unclear whether she even think about the problems.

Two arms wrapped themselves around Fanning's and pulled tight.

"Quickly, mon ami," said Remy into her ear. "We must get inside before they see us."

* * *

Inside Remy's shed the steam gauges showed they were running at full efficiency. Remy had pushed her inside, not too hard, and bolted the door behind himself.

"Here," he said and held out a glass of wine. "Vive la révolution!" Remy scratched his right palm, then lifted his own glass and repeated in English, though French was common enough where

Fanning came from. "To the revolution, my friend, may it never end."

Uncertain how to respond, but not wanting to upset the Frenchman, Fanning raised her glass and took a sip. "Long live the revolution."

Any hope that Remy had not been affected had obviously been in vain, but at least he was not trying to kill her.

"I need to get into the cargo hold," she said. "Without being seen."

"Will you set a bomb?"

"No."

The light in Remy's eyes fell. "We must kill la bourgeoisie."

"We would kill ourselves," she said. "No, Remy, I want to destroy their cargo."

"To bankrupt them and destroy them."

She hesitated. "Yes, that'll be a more fitting punishment."

"How will you get there?"

"I thought you would know."

"We cannot trust the British or any of their allies," said Remy, drawing closer and speaking in lower tones as if they might be overheard.

"You mean Mr Montgomery?"

"Oui, he is a dangerous man."

"So how do I get down there?"

The ship lurched. Remy glanced at the pressure gauges; Fanning followed his gaze. The needles were solidly at full pressure without a flicker. The engines on the port side roared and the ship swung to starboard.

"What's happening?" shouted Fanning as she jumped to her feet.

Remy shouted something in a language Fanning did not recognise; it was not French. The engines shifted direction again.

"Call the captain," said Fanning, pointing at the speaking tube.

"Non!" That was French.

"I'll do it." Fanning grabbed the tube, pulled out the brass whistle, then blew down it hard.

They waited. The ship regained a semblance of stability but still swung under the balloons. Fanning blew again.

"What?" came the tinny reply from the captain.

Then there was a clatter and something at the far end of the tube smashed. The ship swung again; this time the nose tilted upwards but the vessel wouldn't climb unless Remy adjusted the balloons.

Then the background whining of the engines wound down and stopped. The ship swayed in the wind as it drifted.

"How in hell's name do I get down to the cargo hold, Mr Darras?"

6

Early Yesterday Evening

Beatrice had finished introducing Mr Ketteridge to the crew, most of whom were working on the modifications to accommodate the passengers and their cargo. All except Fanning.

"Would you care to come up to the top deck, Mr Ketteridge?"

He smiled. "I'll be happy to go wherever you wish. At least until the sleeping arrangements have been sorted out."

"It shouldn't be much longer," she said and led the way from the bridge into the companionway. "These are crews' quarters and mess—such as it is."

"You sleep here?"

She blushed. "Of course," she said. "I berth with the captain. It is not a large vessel."

Beatrice opened the door to the mess and the galley beside it. The table filled most of the space with chairs crammed in around it.

"I see what you mean," he said. "Very cosy."

"We eat in here but not all together," she said. "There just isn't the space."

"What about our meals?"

"We are having a meal with the captain on the bridge later," she said. "Otherwise they will be brought down to you. Or you can eat up on the top deck if the weather is fine."

That provided a smooth link as they reached the ladder leading up to the top deck. She stood back to allow him to go first.

"After you, Mrs Cameron," he said.

"You are the guest, Mr Ketteridge, you first," she said. She had no desire to have him examining her ankles and lower legs as she climbed. She hoped he did not press the point because it would not be possible to argue without making the reason clear, which would be embarrassing to both of them.

He did not force the issue and climbed.

Beatrice hitched up her skirt and followed. On board she wore fewer petticoats since they made it much harder to get about. The captain wore men's trousers, as did Fanning. Beatrice had thought about it but simply could not bring herself to do it, and cycling bloomers were no longer fashionable.

She accepted Mr Ketteridge's hand as she climbed out of the hatch and stood up on the deck. Ceylon was hotter than she remembered, although it had been several years since she had been here.

"Is it like this on Venus?" she asked. Mr Ketteridge was scanning the horizon. From this vantage point they could see across a great deal of the city to the north wall that separated it from the slums beyond. Nearer buildings blocked their view to the south and west, while Sigiriya itself dominated the east.

"You are from Delhi?"

"Ipswich originally," she said with a smile. "But I have spent the last few years in Delhi."

"Imagine the worst heat and humidity during the monsoon," he said.

She nodded. Summers in Delhi were intensely hot, and the humidity made it almost impossible to maintain any degree of decency. She had frequently had the desire to dispense with her European clothing and turn native. "Venus is like that?"

"Far worse," he said. "It is bad everywhere but in certain parts it is as if the air itself were boiling water."

"I am surprised anyone would want to live in such a place."

"It is a place of wonders, Mrs Cameron," he said. "And, of course, such resources of iron and other commodities that our empire cannot resist."

She realised that he had not, since helping her from the hatch, released her hand and she could feel a curious sensation, a tingling, in it. Somewhat embarrassed she gently pulled away, so as not to imply there was anything unusual or inappropriate.

"The main shed there," she said, indicating the construction in the centre of the deck, "is the steam control room. Monsieur Darras is in charge of our buoyancy." One wide pipe emerged from the deck near the rear and entered the shed. Seven pairs of pipes, one going out and one returning, came from the roof and went out to the seven balloons that lifted the ship. They were inflated now, but as the ship's Faraday was switched off the Beauty remained firmly on the ground.

She looked around, sure Fanning had been up here. She had seen him earlier, but he was nowhere in sight.

"I had hoped to introduce you to Fanning," she said. "But perhaps later."

Mr Ketteridge smiled at her, and there was a hint of something else in his eyes. She looked away quickly. "Being alone with you here is most pleasant," he said.

She felt trapped. Returning down the ladder would be difficult.

Perhaps she could deflect the issue. "I must admit I am curious, Mr Ketteridge," she said, moving away from him to the low rail around the edge of the deck.

"About what?"

"Why you are going to Calcutta, instead of returning directly to Oxford," she said. "Surely you are putting your samples at risk."

"That is quite easy to answer," he said, coming to stand beside her but no longer too close. "The colleges of Oxford and the bequests to the Botanic Garden are, unfortunately, insufficient to fund a trip to Venus of this sort. The doctor was required to find some private support, something I was able to help with. We must visit our most generous patron."

"And what does he get from the trip?"

"This particular gentleman wishes to remain anonymous," he said. "As such, his reward is his own live sample to show off to his friends or keep in secret, just as he chooses."

Beatrice nodded. It was entirely reasonable.

"Are all your samples plants?"

"Plants and fungi, yes," he said. "After all, it is a botanical expedition. Considering the nature of most of the beasts on such a primeval planet as Venus, we would have required a hunter of considerable stature to bring them down. And a much larger vessel than the Frozen Beauty to carry them."

Beatrice had read several novels purporting to tell tales of adventures on the alien planet. "Are there natives on Venus?"

He laughed. "Not that we have found. Nothing with any intelligence to exceed perhaps a dog, and then not even as clever as that."

"I think I should like to visit one day."

"If you do," he said, "I would be happy to arrange the excursion for you."

She turned and smiled. "Shall we go down?"

7

Yesterday Evening

Mr Montgomery was still working on the accommodations with Ichiro so Qi had, reluctantly, asked Mrs Cameron and Fanning to prepare the evening meal for her and their guests. Qi had made a point of ignoring the look Beatrice had given her.

Qi was uncertain what to do about the woman. It was very inconvenient having her aboard but in this instance she had turned out to be useful. Dr Morbury was a very unpleasant person and Qi was glad to be able to delegate the responsibility of baby-sitting him.

They sat around a table that had been brought in from the inadequate mess. The cutlery mostly matched, and Beatrice had unearthed some Chinese-made crockery Qi had completely forgotten they owned. It was classic willow pattern, for export only. It had been part of a shipment her father had carried a long time ago.

Qi had insisted on sitting at the end, facing forwards towards the window. Remy, at the other end, had donated one of his wines, so much better than the drinks they usually had. Fanning was serving and seemed to have some skill in it. Mrs Cameron sat next to the very quiet Dr Lambington—who for all he seldom spoke never ceased to fidget, which was quite distracting.

On the other side were Dr Morbury, opposite Mrs Cameron, and Mr Ketteridge, flanking Qi opposite the restless Lambington. Six of them for a dinner of chicken, potatoes and peas.

"Better than most of what we ate on the trip," said Mr Ketteridge when Qi apologised for the simple fare.

They ate in silence and the awkwardness dragged out.

"Mrs Cameron has been enquiring as to the flora, fauna and fungi of our sister planet, Dr Morbury."

The doctor made a dismissive noise through a mouthful of chicken.

"My knowledge is so unscientific," said Ketteridge. "I thought you might like to enlighten our hosts."

"Really can't imagine where to start," he said.

Mrs Cameron piped up. "Would you say the creatures of Venus are from the same source as us?"

Morbury almost choked. Qi looked up in concern; it would be inconvenient to have a passenger die on them, but the curator was laughing.

It was the timid and fidgeting Dr Lambington who replied. "That is more of a … ah … philosophical question, Mrs Cameron."

"Really?" she said, and let it hang in the air. It was the kind of void a scientist could not resist filling.

"Oh yes," he said. "For us to have a common ancestor there would have to have been some sort of connection between our planets."

Morbury snorted his derision.

"But for anyone to think that, they would have to fail to comprehend the distances involved, Mrs Cameron," said Lambington. "It is quite unthinkable Venusian creatures could have any connection with us, and equally impossible for such life as remains on the Red Planet."

Morbury leaned forwards and jabbed in her direction with his fork. "The planets age like all forms of life," he said. "Mars is the oldest and is in its death throes, while Venus is still young and vital. The age of life upon our planet is in the billions of years. The scope of these concepts is far beyond a woman's capacity to understand."

Qi saw Mrs Cameron straighten and look Dr Morbury in the eye. "My father is a geologist, Dr Morbury," she said carefully. "I have developed an interest in the subject, and it is the opinion of all geologists that the Earth cannot possibly be more than four hundred million years old."

"Ridiculous," said Morbury digging his knife viciously into his chicken. "Geology is not a science, Mrs Cameron. Children playing with stones in the garden." He took a moment to consume a fork's worth of breast. "It is life itself that tells us the age of the planet. Darwin demonstrated the development of life could only occur through natural selection, and that process cannot possibly occur at such a rate."

Mrs Cameron's face was developing an angry shade of red. Rather than let her say something untoward, Qi entered the conversation. "How can you be so sure?"

Dr Lambington shifted in his seat. "Captain, you see, only the tiniest changes can occur from generation to generation, and even then only in some individuals of any given species. Then these changes must be inherited and develop a little more and so on."

Morbury dropped his cutlery onto his plate with a distracting clatter. "The point is this: If life changed at such a stupendous rate, we would wake up tomorrow to find a new and better species of human taking over the world. In fact," he said, "we would not be having this conversation because by now we would all have developed wings and the ability to fly through the Void under our own power."

Perhaps wisely, no one sought to argue. Morbury pushed his seat back and finished off his wine and then held it towards Remy for a refill. Mr Darras gave Qi a dark look and then emptied the remainder of the wine into the doctor's glass.

"As I understand it," said Qi quietly, "life on Venus does not differ all that much from life here."

"Both the bat and the bird can fly," said Morbury. "Even some squirrels and fish can fly. They are not the same. Yes, the animals on Venus have legs similarly jointed to ours. They have skeletons and circulatory systems. There are flowers and creatures similar to insects that perform the same function as pollinating bees and wasps.

"Just because they have developed the same function does not mean they have the same source. Besides, it is on Venus that the fungi have come into their own as the dominant life form. And it is the fungus that we are bringing back."

"How do you mean, dominant?" asked Beatrice, who seemed to have regained control of herself.

It was Lambington who shivered and said, "It's everywhere."

8

Now

The horizon was glowing with the last light of the sun. But for Fanning the sky was below her feet and the sea, reflecting the same rose hue, was above. Quite how she had allowed Remy Darras to persuade her to hang upside-down outside the ship's hull, she was not entirely sure.

She was trusting her life to a crazy Frenchman. He had been pretty crazy even when not under the influence of whatever it was. The question of why she was unaffected still bothered her—along with the idea that perhaps she was affected after all and only thought she was sane.

Did crazy people think they were sane? They probably did.

Rocked by a gust of wind, the ship swung away from her and then returned. She put out her arms to cushion the blow but the hull bludgeoned into her, spinning her away. As she twirled, she caught a glimpse of the length of the vessel and Remy above her.

When she was close to the hull, she was on the border of the Faraday effect; it made her skin feel odd. As she swung away her weight increased to normal. The rope paid out until Remy gripped it harder.

She was almost down to the lowest level.

The idea was that she would be able to peek inside and decide what was to be done. What she wanted was to dump the cargo overboard and never mind the consequences. She had seen the way the dock workers had mishandled the boxes and crates. There was no question they had damaged them and something unpleasant had leaked out.

A fungus.

She had heard Lambington at dinner, but she already knew about Venusian fungus. The scientist who had done this to her and brother had also used fungi. It was in the pamphlets and science journals that he read. The fungus that resembled the human brain and could act like one if given a pattern to follow.

But it was too expensive for him, so he had chosen a different path.

The hull cracked Fanning on the head. She could imagine the sound echoing through the cargo hold and hoped no one would come to investigate. Rubbing her skull, she studied where she was in relation to the ship.

There was one porthole below her. The one she had been aiming for. She looked "down" and saw Remy leaning over the top of the rail. In the fading light, she couldn't clearly see the expression on his face. Somewhere between a grin and a grimace.

She gave him a thumbs-up and he let out the rope again.

And then it was no longer supporting her at all.

As the porthole flashed past, she got the impression of a light inside. She flung out her arms. The sea was a long way below. Her hands dragged along the wood, failing to make any purchase. Her body turned as she fell until she was face down.

Then there was no ship's hull, and only the wide ocean below. Her fingers caught. She gripped reflexively. Her feet swung underneath her and she came to a joint-jarring stop, dangling beneath the Frozen Beauty. Moments later there was a slight jerk around her waist as the loose rope stretched out to its full length beneath her.

From where she hung she could see the thin layer of wood that covered the Faraday grid in the bottom of the vessel. It was painted brightly with the Chinese characters that made up the ship's name. If she were within the Faraday effect this would be easy, but she was not and her full weight dragged on her arms.

Carefully she looked up. She was clinging to a lip running along the lower edge of the hull; there were holes in it at intervals where the Beauty could be tied down if needed. It was solid but her fingers would carry her weight for only so long, and they were already tiring.

The Beauty's engines ran up to speed and she swung as it moved off. Whatever disagreement there had been on the bridge had clearly been resolved.

It was hopeless. She could barely hold her own weight; there were no additional grips that she could see and nowhere to go except down. She adjusted one hand so that the tips of her fingers curled into one of the mooring holes. It was a little firmer like that.

Then she knew what to do. If she failed, she would just fall to her death a little sooner than if she simply hung until her muscles failed. It would mean she would have to grip by one hand for a time, but hope gave her strength.

She looked down at the rope dangling below her. It was long but she didn't have to reel it all in—just enough to get a loop through the hole.

She hesitated. The longer she waited the harder it would be. She took a deep breath, made sure her right hand was firmly hooked into the hole, and then let go with the left. The fingers of her right hand felt as if they would give at any moment.

Reaching down to her waist she found the dangling rope and lifted it. She desperately wanted to hurry but her brother, whispering from the back of her mind, kept her moving slow. She brought her left hand up with the rope, playing through it as she did so.

The weight of it wanted to rip through her fingers but she kept her palm under it. She reached the position where both arms were stretched up and two lengths of rope were in front of her. It was not

so much that her right hand hurt, as that it felt as if it was going
numb and she would fall without realising it was going to happen.

Because only one arm was supporting her and stretched her
shoulder, the other no longer reached all the way to the lip.
Awkwardly she brought the rope down to her face and held it in her
teeth while she made a loop and twisted it, forcing it to bend. Taking
both parts of the loop in her free hand, she lifted it again.

She was able to see the end of the loop through the hole, even
drag it across the fingers of her right hand. There was no way she
could make it bend enough to come down through the hole.
Shooting pains lanced through her shoulder. She could not last much
longer.

Desperately she shoved the loop of rope against the hull above
the hole. Again and again it flipped upwards. She twisted her arm and
tried to get more height as she felt her fingers beginning to slip. One
more shove. This time it slipped down and into the hole. She stared
in disbelief as she shoved more rope and the loop descended several
inches further.

Her right hand could hold on no longer. She released the rope
with her left hand. As she descended the loop went up again. With
one last flail of her left arm, she thrust her hand and then forearm
through the loop before it slid back up through the hole. Her weight
now pulled on both ends of the rope, and she came to a halt dangling
a thousand feet above the ocean.

9

Late Yesterday Evening

The dinner party, such as it was, had broken up. The two scientists had returned to the cargo hold. Dr Lambington had said something about being unwell, which might have explained his restlessness.

Beatrice was standing at the window of the bridge looking out into the night. The dark of the city was highlighted by electric street lamps and punctuated by bright windows. Dominating it all was the Fortress on Sigiriya, ablaze with artificial light.

"May I escort you in a turn around the upper deck?" asked Mr Ketteridge, who had moved up to stand near her—not too close— and also looked out.

Beatrice looked over at him. She was a married woman, and yet not so married since she had left her wastrel husband. Tom Ketteridge was an average-looking man, she thought. Not handsome but certainly not the sort to drive a girl away by his looks.

And he had done interesting things.

"If you promise to tell me of your adventures on Venus, Mr Ketteridge."

"I believe it would be acceptable for you to call me Tom," he said. "May I call you Beatrice?"

She offered her arm by way of acceptance.

Otto was back at his desk working with his notebook and the cards he used to run the Babbage. His face, when he glanced up at the two of them, was glowering. Beatrice allowed herself a slight sigh of confirmation. Otto had taken a fancy to her.

They at least made it to the door with some semblance of propriety but the door and companionway were too narrow to allow them through together. Worse, the ladder to the top deck demanded a complete lack of decorum. But presently they were side by side at the rail in the open.

"Is it true the Venusian fungi can walk and hunt?"

"I believe you have been reading fiction stories, Beatrice," he said, and she could hear the laugh in his voice.

"Is that a no?"

"It is a no," he said with a note of finality. "But, I know where those stories come from."

She waited but he did not seem about to continue. "Tell me, Tom," she said. "You cannot lead a girl up to the edge in that manner and then fail to cross the threshold."

He sighed. "It is not very pleasant."

"I want to know."

"Very well," he said. "It is very common to find the remains of animals completely buried in fungus."

"That does not sound very frightening."

"They are stripped to the bare bone, and usually they are in the process of being digested. It's quite common. Even people have been found," he said. "Of course, the fungus is only a carrion eater, in effect. The creature is killed and the fungus grows on it. Fungi cannot move on their own."

"So what kills them?"

"Oh, any sort of predatory animal, suffocation in a cloud of insects, poisonous plants, even simple heat exhaustion—there are a hundred ways to die on Venus without having to invent walking mushrooms."

"It sounds silly when you say it like that."

"It is."

She did not pull away when he put his arm about her waist.

"There," he said and pointed into the sky. Just above the horizon was a glowing white disk, brighter even than the Victoria Station directly above them.

"So small," she said.

"So very far," he said. "Would you like me to take you there?"

"Could I trust you?"

"Of course."

Beatrice was perfectly well aware that his response had been too slick and too quick. A better man would have hesitated and considered all his misdeeds before answering. A better man might have been honest and said no—and she would have admired him for that.

But this was not the nineteenth century. The old queen was dead and gone. Her son Edward had brought a new decadence to the world despite his age, and he too was dead.

Things were not as they had been in her mother's day. If she wanted to kiss a man who she had only met this very day—though she knew him to be a chancer and even if she was still, technically, married—then she could.

Even if all those things were true… She turned slowly, allowing him to keep his arm about her waist. His other hand reached out and clasped her bare shoulder. She shivered at his touch.

"I'm sorry," he said. "Did I scare you?"

"It's getting a little chill up here now the sun has gone," she said.

He said nothing more but drew her close. She raised her face and looked up at his. He leaned down and kissed her. She felt a tingle as his lips pressed against hers.

She had not kissed any man save her husband before. Tom Ketteridge tasted different. She placed her hand on his arm and felt the muscles beneath his shirt. He was considerably more athletic than her husband.

She blushed and was grateful it was dark enough that he would not see.

"So if you took me to Venus, would you protect me from all the predators?"

"All save one," he said.

"Oh really?" she said. "What is this predator from whom you would not protect me?"

"Myself," he said and crushed her to him, locked his lips with hers. The sensitive flesh of her lips was pressed hard against her teeth and it hurt. His hand slipped to the front of her bodice, he pressed hard and his fingers dug painfully into the top of her breast.

She revised her opinion.

He was arrogant and unskilled in matters of love. The initial attraction evaporated. Unfortunately, he was now thoroughly convinced of her cooperation and she needed to extricate herself from this awkward situation before it went any further.

Her knight-in-armour appeared on deck. "Mrs Cameron?"

Otto! She pulled back and pushed Mr Ketteridge away. Automatically, her hand went to her hair.

"Excuse me, Mr Ketteridge."

She escaped from the rail and stumbled across to Otto. "Did you need something, Otto?"

"Herr Montgomery asked me to inform you that the passenger berths have been completed." Otto spoke in a slightly distracted way, his attention drawn over her shoulder to Mr Ketteridge.

"Excellent news. Thank you, Otto." She turned. "Shall we go down and inspect them?"

She did not wait for an answer but went straight to the hatch and down into the ship.

10

Now

The Beauty increased in speed. Fanning bobbed back and forth on the rope. She managed to wrap the rope around her left leg and foot to provide additional support. By pressing her other foot against the rope she could take the strain from her arms.

She clung to the rope, with her arms wrapped around them. For the time being she felt secure but she could not stay here. If the state of the crew worsened they would probably crash the ship. She had to know what was going on in the hold.

The light of day had faded but the moon would be up soon.

The thrumming of the driving propeller vibrated through the ship. She could both hear and feel it. While she had been on board no longer than Mrs Cameron, Fanning still regarded it as her home—the only home she had had since she had left the southern United States. She did not want to lose it.

She was already tied to one end of the rope. She pulled in the loose end and made a knot so that she was secure. Her arms had recovered sufficiently that she was able to climb, so she passed the end of the rope through one of the other mooring loopholes.

Now, if she fell again, she would not have to worry about the drop, only the pain that the rope around her middle would inflict.

Her eyes had been adjusting with the change in light levels, and the side of the vessel was now highlighted in blacks and whites. With her additional security in place she climbed again, taking care to make as little noise as possible.

She located the small crew-door into the cargo area. It had an external handle that she was able to use as a grip, once she had succeeded in getting her feet onto the lip. She slid herself up the side of the hull by digging her nails into tiny imperfections in the wood to maintain her hold.

She was not planning on opening the door, even if it was unlocked, which it should not be, given that they were in flight. However, there was a porthole beside the door.

Making sure her feet were secure along with her grip on the handle, she leaned across to look in through the porthole. She could not come within six inches of it, even on tip-toe. She was too small.

She moved out along the lip so that she was positioned directly below the porthole. Now she just needed to gain three inches of height.

A high-pitched whine erupted near her head, making her jump. The directional thruster above her and close to the bridge had engaged; steam poured from its exhaust as the turbine spun up to speed.

The Beauty was turning.

Fanning looked down between her feet. There was only the ocean. She had no way of knowing her bearings. The wheeling stars would no doubt have told her, if she knew how to read them. Something was happening on the bridge and she imagined that it could not be a good thing.

She focused on the task she had set for herself. The cargo was the source of the trouble. If she could deal with that then all else would be resolved. She paused and thought of how she would appreciate a pipe of tobacco right now. Smoking helped her to think.

Her other half mocked her. The truth was simple enough. She did not want to go any further. She was afraid of what she might find. When she had been with the scientist, he had talked about the experiments being carried out across the world. He seemed not to comprehend how man's arrogance damned him. He believed he could act without consequence, or failing that, that there was no possible outcome that more science could not deal with.

She and her brother were one of those consequences.

The whine from the thruster unit dropped in pitch and ceased altogether. Whatever their new course, they were now on it. The Beauty swung away from her. As she was on the edge of the Faraday effect, she felt herself increase in weight.

She lifted her right foot and moved it around on the hull until she found the tiniest ledge. She put pressure on it; though it could not be wider than a finger's width her foot did not slip. She reached up with one hand and caught hold of the porthole frame. The Beauty's swing brought it back the other way and she felt the Faraday field sweep through her.

With her new lightness she put her weight on her right foot and lifted herself up to the porthole with almost no effort at all. Her left foot hung free.

Condensation on the outside of the glass, caused by the high temperature within, prevented her from seeing anything but a blur of light and shadow. Taking a chance, knowing that movement would be more noticeable, she released her grip on the porthole and wiped her hand across the glass. It took a bit of scrabbling, but she regained her grip.

For a moment the smeared water vapour was even worse than before but it settled and cleared. She peered inside. The familiar confines of the cargo hold looked normal, save for the modifications that Terry had performed.

The Beauty swung back again and she felt her weight increasing. She clung tightly and hoped her foot would not slip. For the space of ten heartbeats it held firm and the ship commenced its return swing.

Fanning saw a movement by one of the sleeping compartments. The doors were nothing more than draped material, and there was a movement at the bottom of one. She watched as a hand appeared, a head, and then she could see it was Dr Morbury, crawling out of his cubicle.

She watched with the same variety of morbid fascination one has when watching an insect dying. Morbury did not lift his head to see where he was going; he just moved in fits and starts, one limb and then another. It seemed, once or twice, he forgot one. He failed to move a knee on one occasion and it dragged behind. Then he forgot an arm and fell forwards.

Fanning barely noticed as her weight increased and then decreased as the vessel swung back and forth.

The crawling doctor stopped. He coughed. Something grey, about an inch across, was ejected from his mouth and hit the deck where it simply stuck. He coughed again and more emerged.

The arm he had previously forgotten lost its strength and, in the reduced gravity, he rolled over in a parody of a dying fly. She could see his face clearly, or rather she could see the place where his face should have been. His eye sockets were a mass of grey and the flesh of his cheeks partially eaten away, replaced by the same ghastly mass.

Even as she watched the skin of his neck transformed as if it was being eaten from the inside out and converted into a fungoid growth.

He shivered a few times as what muscles were still operable quivered and twitched. Then he ceased to move while the fungus continued to consume him.

11

That Morning

Dingbang woke feeling strange. Sunlight poured in through the porthole of his cabin. He scowled. The ship was light; they must have set off. Why had he not been woken? He sat up and despite the lack of gravity his head spun as if he had stood too fast.

He felt around his head to see if he had been injured but could find nothing. Had he eaten something bad? Had he been ill for days? Had the ship been hijacked?

The last thought lingered. Of all the options, the idea that he had been drugged seemed the most likely. He could have been out for days. They might have killed the rest of the crew—no, that did not make sense. If they had killed the crew, why would they have kept him alive?

But despite his rationalisation he knew there was a reason. They might want him back, and no one else. Least of all Qi.

He let himself down gently on the deck. It was not that his head hurt or even that he felt sick. It was simply that everything about him felt wrong. As if he had the influenza.

He pushed his feet into his sandals and padded to the door but stopped before he reached it on realising he was very thirsty. Returning to the dresser he drained the jug of water he kept for washing. He spilt much of it on himself but downed enough to quench his need for the time being.

If they had intended him to be a prisoner they would have locked the door, but it was open. He peered out carefully. There was no one in sight.

His understanding of the situation was improving as time went on. Clearly Ketteridge was not what he had seemed. He and the others must be Company men who had finally located Dingbang, and this was a ruse to return him to the fold.

And, since Qi's father was dead, they would want Qi as well. They might assume she had been told about the Company. But her father had never told her and indeed had asked Dingbang himself to protect her without giving her that knowledge. It is not a burden she needs, he had said, and Dingbang had agreed.

He slipped from his room. They might keep up the pretence for a while but ultimately the Company would kill all the other crew. This was why they were going to Calcutta instead of London.

If he could raise the crew to mutiny, then throw Ketteridge and the other two overboard, they would be safe. If they could manage it without alerting Qi, so much the better.

Whose help should he enlist? Not Qi, obviously, and Otto was no more than a child. Fanning and Mrs Cameron were of no value in a fight. That left Terry Montgomery, Remy Darras and Ichiro. Ichiro could hear nothing while Remy was an effeminate cockerel.

Terry, then.

The bridge was to the left of his cabin while the way into the cargo hold was to the right. There was no way of locking that door. He needed to get to the engine room which meant either going through the cargo bay or via the top deck.

He went up through the hatch and emerged into the sunlight. The position of the sun suggested it was about ten in the morning. The balloon envelope was taut and he could feel the comforting thrum of the engine in the deck. He headed towards the stern. There was no sign of the Frenchman.

The rear of the Beauty curved in a gentle arc to allow air to flow around the hull and into the huge spinning disk of the propeller.

There was a gap of six feet or so between the stern and the propeller, with a ladder leading down between them. The designers of the vessel had been more concerned with maximising the cargo space for the ice than making it easy to get to different parts of the vessel.

Dingbang threw his leg over the side and, using the railing for support, made his way down. A flat area protruded from the lowest part of the vessel and extended beyond the propeller. It was a continuation of the Faraday grid, to ensure that all the heavy parts of the vessel would be light when needed.

The cargo hold occupied almost the entire lower part of the ship, and the engine room, generators and furnace were on the same level as the cabins and bridge—effectively on the middle deck.

At the rear of the ship a ladder went all the way from the top deck to the bottom. A set of pipes came up over the stern, carrying the super-heated steam from the boilers to the heating elements in the balloons. These were not part of the original design but had been built to Remy's specifications when Qi had invited him to improve the vessel.

Dingbang had not approved of the changes at the time; the pipes did not fit with the aesthetic design and made the ship look ugly. It was not what Qi's father would have wanted. But time had shown the method was very effective. The Frenchman had been as good as his word.

Dingbang descended the ladder, feeling the heat of the pipes against his exposed skin. Halfway down was a hatch that connected to the engine room. It was unlocked, so Dingbang pushed it open and climbed inside.

A wave of heat struck him, far more than he would have expected simply from the furnace. It must be due to the modifications for the cargo.

The first two doors on the left and right were crew quarters for Terry, Ichiro and Remy. The second on the right was the workshop. He went to the door at the end and tried the handle. It turned but the door would not open. The handle itself was hot.

He banged on the door. "Montgomery!" he shouted. He knew the Europeans made fun of him behind his back, about the way he pronounced their names. "Montgomery, it is Dingbang Hsieh. We must talk!"

After a few moments there was the sound of a bolt being drawn back and the door opened. Montgomery was stripped to the waist as usual and covered in sweat. Dingbang was no effete bureaucrat from Peking, but the smell of sweat was overpowering and unpleasant.

Montgomery's arm muscles twitched and it was then Ding noticed the knife in his hand reflecting the red light from the furnace within.

"Who's with you?" Montgomery said, his gaze flicking past Ding into the area behind.

"No one."

Montgomery took a step back to make way for him and gestured with the knife for Ding to enter. Keeping an eye on the blade, Ding came through. Montgomery slammed the door shut and rebolted it.

"Had to be sure," he said. "Can't let them find me."

"Who?" asked Dingbang. Could it be that Montgomery also feared the Company?

"Here," said Montgomery. Ding watched as the man reached down and picked up a length of rope. He tossed it to Ding, who caught it automatically. Montgomery was on him in a second, the knife pressed against Ding's neck.

"Sit down and tie that around your ankles," he said. "Nice and tight."

As Ding let himself down to the floor gently he noticed the bulk of Ichiro in the far corner, trussed up and gagged.

"Sorry," said Montgomery. "But I can't trust you."

12

Now

Fanning stared in horrified fascination as Morbury disappeared beneath the fast expanding fungal growth. She almost forgot she was clinging to the exterior of the ship.

The fact that she was right about the cargo being the source of the problem did not make her feel any better. She wished she could have a smoke.

Then she realised that she could. All she had to do was make her way along the hull to the rear and the open deck section below the propeller.

The ship's oscillations had ceased and she was now only partially within the Faraday. She had to climb down. It was only a few inches but she would have to bend her right leg—which was only supported on a tiny crack in the wood.

It did not matter, she told herself, because she had tied the ropes and she could not fall far if she slipped. Still, the prospect of that did not please her. After all, what if the ropes did not hold? Or the lip broke? Either would send her plummeting to her death.

She took a firm hold of the door handle with her left hand and gripped as best she could with her right on the porthole frame. Tensing herself she bent her right leg. Her left foot was pointed and, as she went down, she used it to search for the lip. Only a few inches, it must be there.

The thruster above her head whined into life again, and the ship swung from under her. Her right hand could not maintain any grip on the frame and she fell. Her left hand tightened convulsively on the door handle, which turned.

Without the slightest click it swung open and she dangled beneath it as a blast of hot air poured out, along with the smell of hot, damp wood.

She got her foot up inside the door frame, and though the door tried to open further as she applied pressure to hold her weight, she managed to keep it from swinging further out. With her other hand she grabbed the frame and pulled herself inside. Her weight disappeared as she moved further in and the whole manoeuvre became easier as she performed it.

She released the outside handle, grabbed the inner one, and pulled it shut. Or tried to. The rope prevented it from closing. She spent valuable seconds pulling it in after her and shut the door.

She had never been so grateful to be inside the ship and safe. As she slid down the door frame and sat, she realised her heart was thumping like a marching band doing double time. It was so hot and damp, her clothes and hair became plastered to her body in moments.

In the harsh electric light everything in the cargo hold was visible. Particularly the remains of Dr Morbury: Almost nothing could be seen of him now save his general outline and his clothes poking through the encroaching layer of fungus.

Halfway across the hold were the boxes of the cargo itself. They looked completely normal. Just wooden crates piled up. If the fungus had escaped from there it must have moved on. It must have eaten Dr Morbury.

Did that mean that Dr Lambington was dead too? And Mr Ketteridge?

Morbury had crawled from his sleeping area nearest to the door, just fifteen feet from where Fanning now sat. The light showed nothing around her, but she moved away from the wall. There might be something hiding in the shadows.

The other two spaces remained a mystery. The men might be in there. They might already be dead. They might just be sleeping. If that was the case she needed to warn them. Either way she needed to get out of here as soon as possible, before the fungus came after her.

Taking pains not to make any sound she climbed to her feet. The background throbbing of the generators and motor that drove the propeller hid small noises, but that worked both ways. Somehow the fungus had managed to creep up on Morbury.

Her mind went back to the way the botanist had scoffed at Mrs Cameron's comments about the fungus attacking people. He was wrong and now the victim of his error. All those skeletons they said they had found on Venus, covered with fungus. Those were not carrion killed by something else, that much was plain.

Well, the Oxford Botanic Garden would need a new curator. If Fanning and the crew managed to get out of this alive she could warn him (whoever he might be) and his people to be more careful with their samples—though she could imagine it would make quite a sight for visitors to see a fungus creeping up on a rat and consuming it while it still lived.

She shivered at the thought.

She needed to move. What if she opened the doors? Clearly it was hot and damp enough in here to mimic conditions on Venus. It seemed reasonable to think the fungus could not survive if it was too cold. She did not think she could get the cargo doors open by herself, but she could at least open the one she had come in by.

After checking the shadows to make sure there was nothing lurking in them, she opened the door again. The incoming air seemed very cold since she had had enough time to acclimatise to the heat of the hold. Getting that door to stay open was another problem.

She found an off-cut from Montgomery's construction work lying in a corner. Cautiously she poked at it with her foot, just in case something was lurking. She wedged it into the door frame. The gap was only a couple of inches but she thought it would hold.

It might reduce the overall temperature by a few degrees.

Fanning took a deep breath. Time to check the other sleeping areas. She gave the fungal remains of Dr Morbury a wide berth but got close enough to see that the surface continued to move as the fungus absorbed his body.

Once she got closer she could hear a faint popping noise coming from the corpse. She could not imagine what might cause it and, after a couple of unpleasant thoughts passed through her mind, she decided that she did not want to imagine—or know for certain, either.

Keeping at arm's length and using another off-cut she pushed back the curtain of the second space. A second pile of fungus, approximately body-shaped, lay on a pallet. She did not know whether it was Ketteridge or Lambington. She did know he was dead.

She inspected the area again, still not seeing any patches of fungus that might attack her. A terrifying thought struck her. She looked up.

The ceiling looked normal. No fungal patches ready to drop on her. She let out a breath she had not realised she was holding.

She made her way towards the stairs that led back up towards the bridge, focused on the need to get to the engine room to turn the heat off.

There was a sound above her. The door to the cargo hold was being opened. Someone was coming in.

Fanning dived beneath the stairs and into the shadow. For a moment she wondered why she did not just talk to whoever it was coming through. But her experiences with everyone else on the ship so far convinced her that, until she knew which way the wind blew, staying hidden was best.

The first voice Fanning heard from the safety of the shadows was Mrs Cameron's.

"Someone's left the door open."

13

Now

The boots of Mr Ketteridge thumped down the steps over Fanning's head while Mrs Cameron's tripped down lightly.

"Wait there," said Ketteridge when they reached the bottom. Fanning shrank back further into the shadows as the man went out across the deck towards the open door. He grabbed the handle and pushed the door wider then kicked the rope out. Fanning watched its length slither over the edge, disappearing faster and faster until the end whipped out into the dark.

The sound of rushing air cut off as he slammed the door shut. She crouched and then knelt in the dark, freezing as his gaze swept the room. He glared into the darkness below the stairs, making her blood run cold and her heart pound so hard she thought he must hear it. Then he looked elsewhere.

"Why are we here?"

Mrs Cameron's words slurred as if she was drunk. Fanning saw her stagger away from the bottom of the stairs.

"What's that?" Beatrice said pointing at the pile of fungus that had once been Dr Morbury. "One of your specimens has escaped. Will it attack?"

Ketteridge came striding back across the deck. "Don't be ridiculous," he said. "You've been told they don't attack."

He caught her by the hand. Fanning was embarrassed by the lascivious look Mrs Cameron gave him. She lifted his hand and entwined her fingers in his. She rubbed her cheek against his hand and then brought it to her mouth. From what Fanning could see she was licking his fingers, all the while looking into his eyes from beneath half-closed eyelids.

She clearly had no idea how to seduce a man. Rather than appearing the coquette, she looked ridiculous.

Ketteridge pulled his hand from her face but did not disentangle their fingers. "Plenty of time for that, Beatrice."

Mrs Cameron pouted and looked around the cargo hold with disdain. "Why are we here, Tom? We would be much more comfortable in my cabin."

"But I have something important to show you, Beatrice, my dear."

He stepped towards the cases piled in the centre of the hold. She did not move for a moment and their arms stretched out between them.

"I don't like it in here," she said. "And I don't think I like you either."

"But you'll still do anything I say, won't you?" he said with an undertone of menace in his voice.

She sighed. "Of course I will."

Fanning frowned. What was wrong with her? Being drunk was one thing but this was more like mesmerism, as if Ketteridge wielded some mystic power over Beatrice. Not that Fanning could understand his appeal at all. They had not even been introduced. The closest they had been since Ketteridge had arrived was at the dinner table when Fanning had been serving.

Ketteridge pulled Beatrice up to the packing cases. "Stay there," he said again and disengaged his hand. Playfully she kept twisting her fingers round his so he could not let go.

He back-handed her across the face. The slap cut like a knife through the hold and threw Beatrice to the floor. She pulled herself into a sitting position and wept noisily, like a child making a point rather than actually being in pain.

Fanning shook her head. This made no sense.

Turning his attention to the boxes, Ketteridge shifted a small one from the top of another and picked up what looked like a chisel from between the packing cases.

The lid of the small crate levered off with almost no effort, as if someone had done it before, quite recently. Ketteridge reached in and pulled out handfuls of straw, dumping it on the ground around him. Then he leaned in and lifted out another box.

The new box was made of a very dark wood bound in brass. It hit the deck with a clunk as Ketteridge put it down. Even under reduced gravity it seemed to possess considerable weight.

Fanning leaned forwards to see better but her view was blocked by cargo. She could only see one end of the box. Still standing, Ketteridge rummaged in his pockets until he found a brass key. He knelt down so only his head was visible but Fanning could see when he lifted the lid.

The actions of Tom Ketteridge had distracted Beatrice from her immature crying. She was now looking at the box and the contents, which Fanning was unable to see from her position.

"That looks horrible," said Beatrice.

"No, it's beautiful," said Ketteridge. There was a tone in his voice that Fanning had only ever heard in church: devout reverence bordering on mania.

"Don't touch it!" said Beatrice.

"That's why we're here, my darling."

"Well, I'm not touching it," she said. "And you can't make me."

She gathered up her skirts, climbed to her feet, and backed away.

Ketteridge stood as well, but slowly. The object he was holding came into view. A livid green under the electric lights, it was a globule of fungus about six inches across. From where she was Fanning could see that the surface was dimpled and patterned, and strands of thin material hung down from it though they were light enough to move in the air. Ketteridge was holding it with his bare hand and a smile touched his lips.

He glanced across to the outer wall where Beatrice had retreated.

"Come here."

"I don't want to."

"Come here, now!"

Fanning was astonished to see the woman's whole body switch from the defiant posture she had been maintaining to one of subservience, with her head down and her shoulders rounded. She shuffled towards Ketteridge.

"That's right," he said. "Do as you're told. It just wants to get to know you."

"I don't want to touch it," she said, returning to the little girl voice.

"I know, but it wants to touch you."

The hackles rose on the back of Fanning's neck. She shifted her position, getting up from her knees and onto her feet. She watched the scene in fascination.

With obvious reluctance but seemingly unable to fight Ketteridge's instructions, Mrs Cameron approached.

Fanning's gaze was attracted by the feathery strands of the green glob. They twitched. She was certain Ketteridge's hand had not moved. They had twitched on their own.

"I'm scared," said Beatrice.

"There's no need."

He reached out his free hand and she stretched out hers until they were touching. She shuffled forwards again. He took a firm grip of her wrist but she did not react to it. Her eyes were fixated on the blob.

There was no question now that it was moving of its own accord—the strands, at least.

Mrs Cameron whimpered as Ketteridge pulled her hand closer to the green mass. The threadlike strands reached towards her.

Fanning screamed her attack.

14

Now

Fanning launched herself from the shadows beneath the stairs.

Ketteridge looked up in astonishment as Fanning rocketed like a banshee, screaming across the deck, bounding fast under the Faraday effect. Whatever spell Ketteridge had over Beatrice appeared to break as she yanked her wrist free of his hand.

Fanning had a plan of sorts. The first part involved her barrelling into Beatrice and knocking her back and away from Ketteridge and his fist full of green. That part worked. Moments later her momentum had transferred to Beatrice who was now flying away from her, though with less speed.

Fanning rebounded a little from the collision and took a moment to orient herself. That moment was all it took for Ketteridge to reach out for her and grab her wrist. He was strong and could easily overpower her small female body.

Ketteridge glanced at the green blob. Its strands had resumed their aimless fluttering.

"It doesn't want me," Fanning said in triumph.

"Of course not," said Ketteridge. "You haven't been prepared."

With an almost casual air he lowered his hand to let the fungus slide off, back into the case where Fanning saw three glass containers held firmly inside. Even in the high temperature of the cargo hold she could feel an even more intense heat radiating from the case. It must have its own heating elements.

Ketteridge was holding her firm, and Fanning used that to lift her feet from the deck and press them into the side of the packing case beside her. She drove her legs straight and shoved herself away from the man in the hopes it would force him to release her.

She failed and instead pulled him with her. Together they flew back towards the stairs. She landed on her back, which would not have been a problem had Ketteridge not landed on top of her, driving the wind from her lungs with his elbow and pinning her legs.

"Fanning, isn't it?" he said. "We haven't been formally introduced. I am Tom Ketteridge, the herald of a new age."

She slapped him with her free hand but he barely seemed to notice. She was not very strong.

As if he were a magician about to indulge in some prestidigitation, Ketteridge showed her his free hand and stretched his arm, thereby pulling the sleeve of his shirt up his forearm. As he splayed out his fingers Fanning could not help but look; the skin of his now-bare wrist had a curious mottled appearance, almost like a faded tattoo.

Ketteridge grinned. As Fanning watched, the tattoo mark darkened and the skin rose in a dozen random pimples. The tip of each pimple darkened and broke open. Thin black tendrils emerged.

Fanning wriggled in an attempt to break free. Ketteridge slammed his palm down on her cheek and forced her head to the side.

She felt an itch in her neck.

Then Ketteridge flew from her. Sideways.

Beatrice stood over them, clutching a chair in both hands. She seemed disoriented. "He hurt me," she said.

Fanning pushed herself up. Ketteridge was crawling a few feet away, shaking his head to clear it. They needed to move right now. She grabbed Beatrice's skirt and used it to pull herself to her feet.

Confused, Beatrice decided to take a swing at Fanning as well, but Fanning saw it coming and ducked. The force of the swing ripped the chair from Beatrice's hand and it flew off over Ketteridge's head, forcing him to duck again.

Fanning knew they had no chance of getting to the door. Ketteridge was stronger than her, and Beatrice was clearly no help since she could not distinguish friend from foe. But they must escape.

Fanning's desperate eye fell on the precious case of fungi, and she recalled Ketteridge's behaviour. She ducked round Beatrice. She gave the case a kick, but whatever it contained to keep it hot was very heavy indeed.

She bent down and got her fingers under the case.

"Beatrice! Stop her!" shouted Ketteridge.

The threat galvanised Fanning and with her fingers under the case she straightened her legs hard, with her back straight, and the case and its contents went flying.

Ketteridge gave an incoherent scream. There was a crash and the sound of shattering glass.

Fanning grabbed Beatrice by the arm and dragged her by sheer force towards the stairs.

Ketteridge did not intercept them. Fanning reached the bottom step and allowed herself a moment to take in what he was doing. As she had hoped, he was busy with the case. He had already got it upright and was casting around for the items to put back.

Fanning pulled on Beatrice's arms, but she was staring at Ketteridge. Fanning slapped her to get her attention and then pulled her up the stairs, round the two flights of metal steps, using her hand on the banister to pull them both up.

They got through the door into the relative coolness of the corridor. Without locks on the doors, there was no way to keep Ketteridge down in the hold.

At the bottom of the ladder she stopped and let go of Mrs Cameron, who seemed to have no will of her own remaining. It had all been exhausted when she struck Ketteridge.

Fanning tried to think what she should do. Her neck itched. Gently she investigated it with her fingertips. There were two or three raised bumps but nothing serious, not even any blood. She rubbed the place, but that just seemed to aggravate the itch. She forced herself to leave it alone.

The question of what on earth she was to do filled her. The problem seemed too big and too complex. She thought through Ketteridge's words and the crew's behaviour.

It seemed that she, Fanning, had been the only one he had not infected—at least until now. That was why she had been unaffected while the rest of the crew had behaved so strangely. Somehow Ketteridge had become an agent of the green fungus, and it was his task to infect them which he did through normal social contact— literal contact.

But that was only the first stage. The second stage required the fungus to infect the victim directly … for what? To make them like Morbury and Lambington, to kill and eat them? No, it had not done that because it remained in the packing case. It was to breed.

They were the birthing ground for new fungus growths and Ketteridge was the means by which the fungus's victims were acquired.

With the rest of the crew almost useless, it was left to Fanning to deal with the problem. She rubbed her neck again. And she needed to do it before she succumbed to the infestation. That the infection might kill them anyway crossed her mind, but at the very least she must stop the fungus from getting to land.

15

Now

Beatrice whined again. She wanted to go back to Tom. "He's a real man," she said. "Not like you, just pretending."

Then she squealed as Fanning's palm stopped just before it struck her cheek.

Spoilt little brat, thought Fanning. Mrs Cameron was not in her right mind, of course, but Fanning could not push away the thought that this faux drunkenness revealed a person's true thoughts. Is that what she truly believes?

Not the time and not the place for such thoughts.

Fanning gathered herself together, took Beatrice firmly by the shoulders, and shook her. "You will not go back to him. You will stay here with me and you will do exactly as I tell you. Or," she paused for emphasis, "next time I will not stay my hand."

Beatrice affected a miserable face.

"Do you understand, Beatrice?"

She nodded sullenly.

"Very well, we will find Remy and … you can play with him."

Beatrice brightened. "Will he speak French?"

"If you ask him nicely," said Fanning. "Now come along. Look lively."

She went to the base of the ladder, pulling Beatrice after her. She placed her directly beneath it. "Up you go, girl."

"Tom wanted to look up my dress," said Beatrice. "Do you want to look up my dress?"

"I want you to get up there as quick as may be, or I'll tan your hide, Miss."

Beatrice climbed without a further word.

Fanning glanced in both directions before she followed. Forwards to the bridge where Qi and Otto had stopped shouting; and back to the stern where Ketteridge would probably soon have rescued his precious masters and be on her tail once more.

Beatrice was dawdling. Fanning gave her a slap on the ankle. "Ow."

But she moved faster and Fanning followed. Fanning noticed she could see halfway up Beatrice's elegant calf before the rest was lost in shadow. Part of her admired the view.

"Can you see up my dress?"

"I'm not looking."

"I bet you are." Beatrice continued to climb. In fact she stretched to take the steps two at a time, revealing considerably more of her lower limbs than could possibly happen by accident.

Fanning shook her head. If the woman had not been intoxicated, she might have taken advantage of the invitation.

The air on the upper deck was cool and fresh. A quick glance around the horizon showed they were somewhere in the middle of the ocean. But only Qi and Otto would have a clue as to where, exactly.

The moon had risen. No airships smaller than a British Sky-Liner or a German Zeppelin flew through the night. It was too dangerous. But here they were, thousands of feet up in the clear night. The engine throbbed, the propeller thrashed the air, while the wind sighed through the rigging of the envelopes and steam hissed through the pipes.

"It's so beautiful," said Beatrice turning round and around looking up into the sky filled with stars and the Milky Way a strip across it.

"Sure is," said Fanning. But they had no time for that.

Fanning went to Remy's shed and pushed at the door. It would not open. Fanning banged on it.

"Remy! Let us in."

"Remy is not here," came his voice from within. Fanning looked heavenward as if for guidance, or help. Or perhaps a lightning bolt to end all of her troubles permanently.

"Vive la révolution, Remy. J'ai besoin de votre aide, mon ami."

"You can speak French too!" said Beatrice in delight. Fanning ignored her.

There was a pause and the door unbolted. Remy's hand reached out to grab her and pull her inside, but Fanning evaded it. "Listen, Remy, you must protect Beatrice. The British scientists wish to perform unspeakable acts upon her."

"Mais non!"

"Oui, vraiment."

He pulled the door open but kept himself hidden behind it. "I will keep her safe," he said. "Send her in."

Beatrice was staring up at the stars again, Fanning took her by the hand and guided her inside.

"Lock the door, Remy," Fanning said. "It is not safe."

Remy went to close the door but Fanning put her hand against it. "The Beauty needs to descend, but gently so no one notices."

Remy nodded. "I will do it," he said. "Bon chance, et behatzlacha."

The door closed on Fanning's confused face: what on God's green earth was behatzlacha? Was Remy too far gone? Had she just made a terrible mistake in entrusting Beatrice to his care? What if they became violent like Qi and Otto?

There was no time to worry. Fanning paused to look at the balloons. There was no way to know if Remy had remembered to carry out her instruction just by looking at them.

Fanning turned towards the stern. The next part of the plan required her to enter what could be a lion's den. Montgomery had been a soldier and could be very dangerous, or as a pliant as a kitten.

It took Fanning less than half a minute to make her way to the ladder in the stern and climb down to the door. She went through and stopped in front of the engine room door.

After the coolness of the outside air the heat in the passage was oppressive, and it was going to get worse. The noise, filtering through the grill above the engine room door, was far worse too, with the thumping and hissing of the boiler, pumps and engine along with gears grinding one against another. There was little risk of being heard.

She looked at the three doors. It was not wise to leave unchecked rooms behind her; there might be someone, or something, lurking inside waiting for her to pass and then sneaking up behind.

The first door she opened stealthily. The room inside was tidy to the point of obsession. Terry's cabin. The bunk was made; there were no personal possessions on show and nothing to distinguish this space from any other. No hint of personality except a single bell hanging in a wooden frame in the centre of the small table and a metal clapper resting in a hook with it. It swayed a little with the movement of the ship.

The room opposite was similar in its sparseness, but there were charcoal sketches on the wall. Paper and drawing implements lay on the table in a casual tidiness. One image in particular caught her attention: It was her own face caught in a serious moment of contemplation. All the other crew were there too, each one drawn with a sure delicacy.

Fanning left Ichiro's room filled with astonishment. She did not think anyone knew that he drew. She did not understand why someone with such talent would keep it hidden away. Curiously she felt her desire to succeed in her mission redoubled; she did not want to see Ichiro's talent destroyed.

The third door was locked. She knew that was for equipment. Pity, she could have done with something heavy to hit with.

She faced the entrance to the engine room. Despite the temperature here she could feel the greater heat from the door itself.

She tried the handle.

16

Now

The handle turned but the door did not budge.

Fanning took a step back. She must gain entry somehow. She glanced again at the workshop door. There would be tools in there, but they were as inaccessible as the engine room.

She studied the door once more, and the grill above it that carried the heat and noise from inside. A wooden grill set into a wooden frame that might, just possibly, come free.

Under the effects of the Faraday it was a simple matter to jump up onto the door handle and grab hold of the grill. The noise level increased and she found herself breathing air that was so hot she might as well have been inhaling the super-heated steam for the balloon heating elements.

She peered through the wooden slats. The view provided was not complete; she could not see directly below her, but the opposite side of the engine room was clear enough. The furnace and boiler occupied the far side; the iron hatch to the fire was shut.

There were two pairs of feet: the pair on the right were very large and wearing sandals. Ichiro. There was a binding around the ankles. So he was no concern.

The pair to the left wore heavy boots and were not bound. That had to be Montgomery. But in that position, although she could see nothing of his upper body, he would be able to see her clearly coming through the grill.

He might be asleep. She imagined that in this heat it would be hard to stay awake. When they were in flight, he and Ichiro often went up on the top deck.

She focused on the wooden slats that made up the grill. The frame was part of the main structure of the door so the slats would have to be removed one at a time.

Each slat was about one quarter of an inch thick and separated from the next by a gap of an inch and a half. They were angled downward towards her, which was the main reason her view of the interior was obscured. The slats were in grooves angled up and into the engine room. If there was nothing to prevent it, they should slide up and out.

She could not tell if the pieces had been pinned or nailed in place but the varnish used to coat the whole grill showed no break where the slat met the frame. It was as good as if they had been glued into place. She tried to move a slat but it was solid. At the very least she needed something to break the varnish coating.

She jumped down lightly. The air was noticeably cooler at this level. She thought for a moment and then hurried back to Terry Montgomery's room. It felt sacrilegious but she went inside and took the bell hammer from the table. The handle was a thin iron rod.

Although it was hard to tell the true weight of things in reduced gravity, she had learnt the skill of moving an object in the air. Its resistance to the movement helped you judge its real weight. The hammer was heavy for its size.

As she exited Terry's room she had another thought. She needed to make the Beauty as cool as possible, so perhaps she could open the stern door and keep it that way.

In Ichiro's room she found one of his belt-ropes. She took it and went to the rear end of the passage.

Fanning tied the rope to the handle on the inside and then pushed it open. It was completely dark outside, but the ocean reflected the silver of the waxing half-moon. The cool air was refreshing. She had not realised just how tiring it had been in the heat.

She stared at the ocean for a long moment and then realised their altitude was considerably less than it had been. Remy had remembered. It was difficult to judge height over the sea and she had no idea how much time they had before they hit. Either she would deal with the problem or they would all drown, taking the Venusian fungus into the depths.

The pipes carrying steam up to the balloons were perfectly placed. She threaded the rope through and tied it off so that the door was now flung wide and would stay that way. It might help.

She took the bell striker from her pocket and went back to the door. She jumped up again. Choosing the highest slat she scraped around where the varnish glued it to the frame. It cracked easily.

Encouraged, she worked all the way around the slat, although the inner part was awkward. The curve in the handle proved a boon. Doing the other end, nearest her head, was harder because she could not see what she was doing, but eventually she was satisfied.

She pressed against the slat. The far end moved a little. She knew that both would have to move together or it would get jammed. Taking a chance she hit the heel of her hand in a sharp blow against the stuck end.

It shifted. She gripped the middle of the slat and pushed it up. It slid along its grooves, sticking every now and then but she was satisfied it would come out. Carefully she put it back in position. She would not remove it completely until she was ready.

The second slat came loose as easily as the first. She decided she did not have time for another. If she had been in her brother's body instead of the other way around, she would not have been able to get through.

She placed the bell striker in her pocket and removed the first slat. She tossed it back and out of the ship through the door. She watched it fly back and into the propeller, which chewed it to splinters. She took out the second one and did the same.

Grabbing the third slat, still stuck in place, she pulled the front half of her body up. In order to surprise anyone inside she gave herself a push that sent her flying through the gap.

Two facts struck her at about the same moment. One was that it would probably have been better if she had gone through the gap face up, and the other was that she was going down headfirst on to a fully awake Dingbang Hsieh lying directly in front of the door.

17

Now

Even falling at the Faraday-reduced speed there was nothing she could do to stop herself landing on Dingbang. In the time she had available during her descent she saw that the first mate was not tied up, as Ichiro was. That made it even more surprising that he did not attempt to move as she came crashing down on him.

She threw her arms above herself and her hands hit first; she managed to place them to either side of his knees. However, she was no acrobat and although she succeeded in preventing herself from landing on him directly, she toppled towards the door and her knees struck him in the face.

He made no sound. She finally came to rest lying half across his lap. She bounced to her feet expecting an attack from either Dingbang or Montgomery.

She glanced round. Montgomery's eyes were also open, but he too was not moving. She looked over at Ichiro. He was awake but tied up. All their eyes had the same open irises that came with the crazy.

Taking care that she could jump away at the slightest sign of danger, she knelt at Dingbang's side. His skin was mottled and discoloured around his neck and face. She pulled back the sleeve of his jacket to reveal fingers, hand and wrist with the same unnatural patterning. She did not touch his skin.

Fanning knew that Dingbang had been the person to find Ketteridge and had offered the services of the Frozen Beauty to carry the cargo. That would mean that he had been the first to be infected.

And this was the result. After the disorientation and strange behaviour came paralysis.

Seems that would mean that Montgomery was infected soon after Dingbang, unless the degree of hard work he had engaged in had accelerated the effect. Fanning knew that snakebite venom spread faster when a person was agitated. Perhaps this was the same.

No one was stoking the furnace and that meant they would lose pressure. Fanning did not want to die, but if killing Ketteridge and this fungus meant drowning them all in the ocean, that was what she would do.

Handles controlled valves on the pipes that led up to the balloons. She decided not to close them. Remy had already started the process at his end. He knew what he was doing, even in his confused state. She did not know what effect closing them at this end would have.

The new pipes leading down into the cargo hold were obvious, along with the hole that had been made through the deck to accommodate them. She moved across to the newly cut access, got down on all fours, and peered down.

Several layers confronted her: first, the one-inch-thick wooden deck itself and then a six-inch layer of some woollen substance. She did not think it could actually be wool from an animal but it had that appearance. Next came a thin wooden layer that supported the wool, a gap of three more inches and finally a double thickness of one-inch wood with a half-inch gap between.

The wool must provide the primary insulation to prevent the heat of the furnace reaching the cargo hold that would normally be filled with ice.

Most of the space was occupied by the heating pipes but between them she could see the deck of the hold about ten feet below. The heat coming from the pipes warmed her cheeks. She looked but there were no control valves for these pipes. It seemed Montgomery and Remy had not considered it of sufficient importance since they would be dismounting the system as soon as the journey was complete.

Fanning studied the gap around the pipes. It would be a squeeze and touching the pipes would be very painful. She could hold her hand no closer than an inch before it became too hot. At a guess that would be all the space she had.

There was no need to tie back her hair. Before the experiment her hair had reached all the way down her back, thick and strong. Frank did not like being in a girl's body; he had insisted she cut it short. She took a deep breath. In this instance going head first would be better so she could see what she was getting into. And on this occasion there was no risk of falling to her death.

Just suffering severe burns and perhaps being murdered by Ketteridge. Or worse, getting turned into fungus food. She reminded herself she already was.

There was the question as to what happened after the paralysis stage. What happened to the victim then? Maybe they just died anyway.

With that comforting thought she lay down by the hole, stretched her hand down into it, tucked her head in and wriggled her way inside.

The heat against the back of her head and shoulders was intense. This was the hardest part as she had to bend her body into the gap. The smell of burning hair hit her nose. There was nothing she could do about it. More of her body came over the edge and the weight on her arm increased.

She brought her other hand round and brushed the back against a pipe. Searing pain shot through her and she bit down on the cry of agony that wanted to explode from her lips.

Keeping her fingers on the wood lining that composed the roof of the cargo hold she let herself drop further. The smell of burning fabric now filled her nostrils, but she had no idea what was touching the pipes.

She descended further and her head popped out into the hold. The noise of the engine room diminished.

The sound of a solid thump reverberated through the hold but the source was behind her head.

"Christ!" muttered Ketteridge. "Stop fighting, you bitch."

He made the sound of someone having the wind knocked out of them. Fanning twisted her head to see the upside-down image of Ketteridge slamming the captain's head into the deck. Qi lay on the deck with her hands tied.

This did not stop her from jerking her head free, slamming both fists into Ketteridge's face and twisting so she could kick him in the thigh with her bound feet. He staggered back, recovered his balance and kicked her in the head. Blood bloomed from her nose.

"We mustn't be late!" said Qi, then coughed. "We have a cargo to deliver."

Ketteridge had his back to Fanning.

She let go, deciding a momentary brush against the scorching heat of the pipe would be a small price to pay. She dropped to the deck.

18

Now

Fanning's fall took two agonisingly long seconds under reduced gravity. And for all that time she thought Ketteridge would notice her and turn. But there was no reason why he should. Her fall made no sound.

As the deck approached she stretched out her arms just as she had falling from the door in the engine room. This time there were no obstructions. She absorbed the speed of her fall and bent her arms. She brought her legs down and finished her silent fall on all fours with barely a bump.

Fanning looked up at Ketteridge and the captain. Qi was face up and he had his foot on her neck. She writhed this way and that, but with her hands and feet tied she was unable to escape.

Though he had her pinned he was still able to use his hands and was in the process of opening up the special brass and wood box. The captain's thrashing weakened and her face was very pale. Paler than usual—Ketteridge was strangling her.

Even if it was possible to survive the initial infection, Fanning knew the second one was fatal. She glanced across at the grey mound that had once been Dr Morbury. Some parts were gaining a greenish hue as if it was maturing.

First things first. Stop the captain from getting infected.

Ketteridge reached into the opened case as Fanning took a short run and flung herself at his head. She had no particular plan in mind, other than stopping him from infecting the captain and getting his foot off her neck.

Fanning slammed into him. He carried a lot more mass than her slim frame, but he was not expecting the attack and she was moving fast. Fanning wrapped her hand round his neck, as she flew into and past him. The sudden addition of her weight and velocity pulled him off balance.

The jar of fungus slipped from his fingers. As she knocked him to the side, across Qi, they both watched the inexorable descent of the glass container. It hit the deck and shattered. Green fungus spread out across the deck, perilously close to the captain's head. Tendrils, freed from the container, tasted the air.

Ketteridge twisted as they fell together so she was under him as they landed, both of them face up. He jerked his head back and slammed it into her solar plexus, knocking the wind out of her.

He pushed himself up on to his knees and turned.

"You!"

She pulled her legs back and slammed her feet between his legs. She must have missed. He fell back and flailed with his arms to keep his balance, but he was not writhing in pain. Fanning was pushed faster in the other direction and ran into something soft.

She screamed and rolled away from the remains of Dr Morbury, frantically brushing at her hair trying to dislodge the sticky remains. She hoped it was not capable of growing tendrils yet. Well, even if it was…the cargo hold seemed to tilt and she staggered. She saw that Ketteridge had not staggered. He had tilted with the ship.

She rubbed her eyes. And giggled. Something inside shouted at her to pull herself together. She focused on Ketteridge with difficulty.

"Having problems?" he asked, his voice booming in her ears. "Come here, Fanning."

Her left foot moved forwards, she frowned at it. "Stop that, you're not going anywhere," she said and the foot moved back under her.

Come on, Liza, wake up.

She looked around for her brother. He wasn't there. She shook her head, she lost her balance, staggered back and came up against the door. The captain was going to get the second dose. Fanning had to move, had to get past Ketteridge.

The door, Liza.

She wished he'd stop pestering her. He was always telling her what to do, always wanted his time in charge. It was her goddamn body. He had no right to it.

She felt behind her.

"Come here, Fanning."

Don't do it.

"Go to hell," she said to both of them.

"There's no hell, Fanning."

She looked up at Ketteridge. There were two of them; she straightened up her eyes and the two merged into one. He was walking towards her.

"There's only death."

He reached out for her.

Fanning gripped the handle of the door behind her, and turned it. Ketteridge put his hand on her shoulder. She brought up her other hand and held his tightly against her. She pushed back, the door opened, and she fell with it, pulling Ketteridge with her.

Her arm twisted awkwardly as she clung to the handle. Ketteridge followed her out and true gravity took hold of them both. Fanning pulled his hand from her shoulder.

"No!" he cried as he fell past her. He tried to grab her and she felt his fingers run the length of her body, catching momentarily on folds of cloth that he could not grasp.

She heard the splash.

Looking down, she noted they were barely twenty feet above the surface of the sea.

Fanning had been ready to breathe a sigh of relief but there was no time. They would hit the water within minutes and that would be the end of everything. So that would be all right.

Goddamn it, Liza Fanning, get your behind in motion. You want to kill your brother?

Fanning shook her head. She hated her brother; she could just let go and fall herself. What would he do about it then?

She did not let go.

She lifted her dangling feet and got them on to the deck, then arched her body until most of it was balanced inside. She pushed against the door and forced herself into the hold.

The captain was moving but Fanning could see a line of tendrils crawling across the floor in her direction. Not waiting to close the door, she launched herself once more across the deck. This time she stopped by the captain's head and prepared to stomp on the tendrils.

No, Liza, they'll get you instead.

She took hold of the captain's bound wrists, yanked her from the ground and sent her flying across the hold towards the stairs. Those tendrils are really quite pretty. She smiled; it would be so nice just to pick them up and put them back in their little pot.

We're going to crash, Liza.

19

Now

Fanning staggered away from the fungus with its delicate and tantalising tendrils. She focused on the captain. They had to get the heat back into the balloons so the ship did not crash.

The knots around the captain's hands were tight and took a great deal of concentration to undo. Qi's eyes opened as Fanning worked at them.

"Fanning."

"Yes, Captain."

"You need to hurry up."

"Yes, Captain."

There was a pause as Fanning managed to pull an end of rope through, though it did not seem to help a great deal.

"Mr Ketteridge?"

"Overboard."

"He was trying to stop me delivering the cargo."

Fanning paused at the curious comment. Every time Fanning's mind wandered her nagging brother would yell at her from the back of her mind, keeping her on track.

If the ship goes down the cargo won't be delivered.

"The ship is going down, Captain."

"What? Why?"

"Mr Darras shut off the heat."

"Mutineer!"

"No, Captain, he thought he was doing the right thing."

She unthreaded another end and the rope came loose. The captain pulled her hands free. She ran her hand across her forehead where her straight black hair was matted with blood.

"Darras is a fool, I'll tell him."

"Let me untie your legs."

The rope binding the captain's ankles presented less of a challenge and as soon as Fanning was done Qi bounded to her feet. "I'll be having words with Remy Darras," she said as she headed up the stairs.

She paused at the top. "Fanning!"

"Captain?"

"Get that door closed and tidy up in here, it's a mess."

"Yes, Captain."

Once Qi was gone Fanning looked around. She desperately wanted to clean up as the captain said. And get the fungus back in its jar where it would be safe. She wanted to touch it.

But her brother would not let her.

Under his instruction she pulled open the remaining boxes, taking care to avoid the creeping horror on the floor. Instead she covered it with straw and bits of wood. She did the same with the makeshift cubicles constructed by Montgomery, disassembling them and piling up the pieces on the remains of Morbury and Lambington.

Then she extracted her matches and set light to it all.

Even in her confused and biased state she was aware that setting a fire inside the ship was not the very best idea. But her brother could see no other solution. They could not toss the fungus into the sea. It might survive. And it was too dangerous to be permitted to remain.

So, in spite of the flames, Fanning stayed with the fire, keeping it under control and ensuring it did not spread. She watched as the fungus dried in the heat, ignited and was consumed until only cinders remained.

As each was destroyed she extinguished the flames by spreading out the burning embers and stamped them into dust. She destroyed it all.

Through the haze of her confused thoughts she noted that they had not landed in the ocean. Her brother kept at her from the back of her mind, forcing her to remain focused on the task, not letting her sleep which she desperately wished to do.

Not until the last of the cargo was cremated, her pretty fungus was no more and the fires were all out. Choosing a corner the furthest from the stairs and the burnt-out embers she curled up and her brother went quiet.

* * *

Fanning opened her eyes and stared at the ceiling. The ship was not swaying and she was at full weight. The porthole of her cabin was open and the mixed cacophony of a city filtered in, along with a moist heat.

She pulled the sheet from over her and stepped awkwardly down to the deck. She realised she was clean and the clothes that hung over the back of the chair were the same.

Her head was clear but she could remember every detail of the events with Dr Morbury's cargo. Every single one.

She raised her fingers to her neck where she had been pierced by Ketteridge's tendrils but could feel nothing. She put on the clothes; the trousers, shirt and waistcoat provided a form of armour she could use against the world.

She was filling her pipe when there was a knock at the door.

Beatrice Cameron came in. She was wearing her smile and carrying a cup of tea.

"I'm glad to see you're up," she said. "You were unconscious for so much longer than the rest of us. We were worried."

"Everyone is all right?" said Fanning, laying aside her pipe and taking the tea. It was strong and slightly sweet, just the way she liked it.

"We are, though embarrassed by the whole affair."

Fanning shook her head. "Ain't nothing to be ashamed of," she said, "none of us were in our right minds."

"Except you," said Beatrice. "We are all in your debt."

"Captain going to throw me off for destroying the cargo?"

Beatrice laughed. She had a sweet laugh. "Oh no, the captain knows you saved her life in particular as well as the rest of us."

Fanning nodded and took another mouthful of tea.

There was a crash from somewhere in the ship. Fanning frowned.

"Remy and Terry are removing the heating pipes. And Ichiro is scrubbing the decks with carbolic."

"No more Venusian plants then?"

Beatrice shook her head. "No, Captain says from now on, just ice."

~ end ~

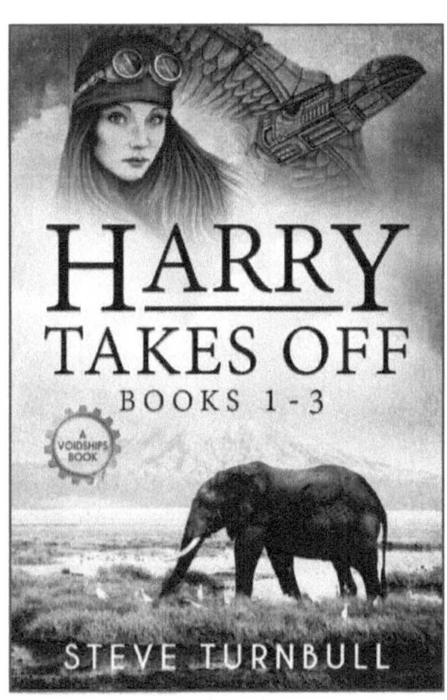

Harry Takes Off

1896. Trouble in Zanzibar? The Edgbaston Sisters to the rescue.

Harriet and Khuwelsa are teenage sisters and they love flying over the grasslands in their flying machine: The Pegasus. But East Africa is a cauldron of political tensions as the global empires of Britain and Germany vie for control.

http://bit.ly/harry-01

For all Voidships books, join the mailing list at:

http://bit.ly/voidships

Steve Turnbull was born in the heart of London to book-loving working-class parents in 1958. He lived with his parents and two older sisters in two rooms with gas lighting and no hot water. In his fifth year, a change in his father's fortunes took them out to a detached house in the suburbs. That was the year *Dr Who* first aired on British TV, and Steve watched it avidly from behind the sofa. It was the beginning of his love of science fiction.

Academically Steve always went for the science side, but he also had his imagination—and that took him everywhere. He read through his local library's entire science fiction and fantasy selection, plus his father's 1950s *Astounding Science Fiction* magazines. As he got older he also ate his way through TV SF like *Star Trek*, *Dr Who* and *Blake's 7*.

However, it was when he was 15 he discovered something new. Bored with a maths lesson, he noticed a book from the school library: *Cider with Rosie* by Laurie Lee. From the first page he was captivated by the beauty of the language. As a result he wrote a story longhand and then spent evenings at home on his father's electric typewriter pounding out a second draft, expanding it. Then he wrote a second book. After that he switched to poetry and turned out dozens, mostly not involving teenage angst.

After receiving excellent science and maths results, he went on to study computer science. There he teamed up with another student and they wrote songs for their band, with Steve writing the lyrics. However, they admit their best song was the other way around, with Steve writing the music.

After graduation Steve moved into contract programming but was snapped up a couple of years later by a computer magazine looking for someone with technical knowledge. It was in the magazine industry that Steve learned how to write to length, to deadline, and to style. Within a couple of years he was editor and stayed there for many years.

During that time he married Pam (who also became a magazine editor), whom he'd met at a student party.

Though he continued to write poetry, all prose work stopped. He created his own magazine publishing company which at one point produced the subscription magazine for the *Robot Wars* TV show. The company evolved into a design agency, but after six years of working very hard and not seeing his family—now including a daughter and son—he gave it all up.

He spent a year working on miscellaneous projects including writing 300 pages for a website until he started back where he had begun, contract programming.

With security and success on the job front, the writing began again. This time it was scriptwriting: features scripts, TV scripts and radio scripts. During this time he met a director, Chris Payne, who wanted to create steampunk stories, and between them they created the Voidships universe, a place very similar to ours but with specific scientific changes.

With a whole universe to play with, Steve wrote a web series, a feature film, and then books all in the same Steampunk world and, behind the scenes, all connected.

Join the mailing list at http://bit.ly/voidships